Last Stand at the Brain Shop

Three Tales from the Four Horsemen Universe

Robert E. Hampson

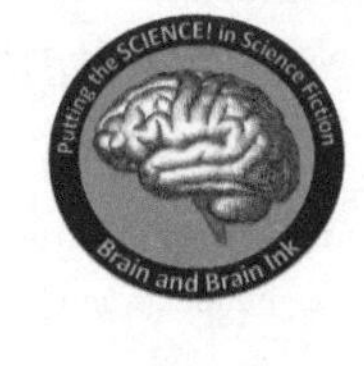

Brain and Brain Ink

Contents

Dedication

For Ruann, the love of my life; for Mom, my first fan; and for Dad, my hero and role model.

Additional Copyright Information

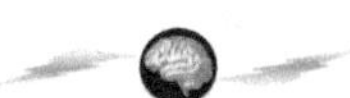

HEADSPACE AND TIMING

"No shit, there I was. Murthering great battle on Orkutt and my head's up goes red and I see the warning 'Critical systems failure. Communication lost, Pinplant T00A7. Emergency eject.'"

The four men were clustered around a small table at the bar. Tall glasses half-filled with beer in front of three of them and shorter glass with a dark amber liquid in front of the fourth. The pitcher of beer was half-full and the storyteller, Ginzberg, grabbed it and refilled his glass.

"I hated those damned models. Give me a Mark Seven with full combat overrides." The new speaker, Jackson, refilled his own glass, emptying the pitcher in the process.

The third person at the table only grunted and muttered under his breath.

"Wait," said the fourth person at the table. It was the newbie, Kaizo, or Kaishwan, or something like that. (The others just called him Kaiju since he was new and hadn't earned a regular team-name yet.) "Did he just say 'chicken pluckers?'"

"Yeah, Angus swore off swearing after that last battle." Jackson supplied.

"Um, why did he swear of swearing?" Kaiju asked. "And how did he do that anyway if he can just mutter and make it *sound* like he was swearing in the first place?

The object of his curiosity just muttered again. "Not our story to tell, kid," Jackson translated.

"Yeah, in this crowd, if a merc doesn't volunteer his story, you don't ask," Ginzberg interjected. "Besides, you have to earn the right to hear it." He picked up the pitcher and looked pointedly at the kid. "Speaking of which, junior buys the drinks."

"Oh, hell no." Kaiju responded. "I know my rights. I know how to earn his story, too." He reached into a pocket and pulled out a shiny coin, rapped it on the edge of the table, then laid it flat on the surface of the table. It was hexagonal, with the image of a man on horseback.

"Nice one, junior, so shiny. Which means it's new, like you." Jackson pulled out a well-worn coin with a German eagle on the face, as did Ginzberg. Angus grunted, dug deep into his pocket and pulled out a silver coin with lettering on it. The silver was blackened with age, but the lettering was crisp and clear: 'C-H-A-O-S.'

"What does that mean?" Chagrinned, Kaiju put his coin back into his pock-et.

"It means Angus is an old soldier." The bartender raised his voice to be heard across the room. It wasn't hard; the room had been quiet except for slight rustling sounds ever since the kid rapped the table. "He was given that coin by the man they used to call 'Mad Dog.' It also means that you need to learn a bit more about the challenge coin tradition, kid." He spread his arms and indicated the rest of the inhabitants in the room. In front of every single patron was a coin, shiny or tarnished, the entire tavern had responded to the call.

"I don't see his." Kaiju pointed to another grizzled veteran sitting at the bar.

"I did," the bartender replied, and several patrons nodded. "You don't just wave a DFT around."

"DFT? What's that?" Kaiju's eyes went wide. "You mean *he's* got a Depi—..."

"Just stop right there, kid. You don't just call out the name in public, either." Jackson had put his hand on the kid's arm. Ginzberg had a hand up as if to cover the kid's mouth and a rather wicked-looking knife had appeared in Angus' hands. "Just...leave it. Besides, you made the call, and everyone in the room produced their coin. That means you buy the drinks...for everyone."

"Oh. Oh, shit," the kid said, but he pulled out his Yack, checked the balance, then nodded to the bartender.

Once the pitcher had been refilled, and Angus had a fresh glass of whisky, Ginzberg resumed his story. "See, told ya, kid. I'll tell my stories for free, just buy my beer. Now, where was I?"

"He was on Fors, getting ejected from your CASPer," Jackson whispered to the kid.

"I thought it was Orkutt?" Kaiju whispered back.

"Doesn't matter, it changes each time, just listen."

"So, there I was, no shit. Big honkin' battle on Kr'ss-9 and my head's up goes red and I see the warning 'Critical systems failure. Communication lost, Pinplant T00A7. Emergency eject.'"

"Hated those suits," added Jackson. Angus just mumbled about rams and ruck marches.

"Ejected right onto the battlefield, buck naked."

Kaiju held up a hand and interrupted. "Whoa, what did you do?"

Jackson grinned, and gestured at Ginzberg with his beer, sloshing a bit on the table in the process. "Dude, you had your haptic suit on."

Kaiju snickered. Angus snorted and went back to his whisky.

Ginzberg glared at the other three. "Sure, so I was the next best thing to buck naked, in the middle of the battlefield."

"Wool shirts. It launched you 2 miles to toward the rear lines." It was the first time Angus had spoken clearly. Perhaps the whisky was loosening him up.

Kaiju's expression was all screwed up as he tried to parse the meaning. He was mouthing the word 'wool' when Jackson leaned over and whispered, "Wool shirts. Bull shit. I guess it makes sense if you're Angus."

Ginzberg focus his glare on the Scot. "Rear lines my ass, I hit the ground right in the front of a charging Oogar screaming at me. The whole time I keep hearing 'Critical systems failure. Communication lost, Pinplant T00A7.' So, I can't even open a link to call for help!"

Angus snorted, and went back to staring into his glass.

Kaiju was still working through what he'd heard. "Wait, pinplant A7? That's like..." It was obvious he was trying to calculate a number.

Jackson saved him the effort. "One hundred sixty-seven, Kid. It's Hex."

"Wow, Ginzberg! You were one of the first to get a pinplant? What was it like?"

"Oh, it's worse than that. Jackson drained his glass with a gulp, and refilled it from the pitcher. He looked at Ginzberg, and knowing the story that was to come, topped his off as well and motioned toward Kaiju. "Oh yes, it was worse than that, kid, they started the numbering at Ay-Zero. Slick here was number seven."

"Oh, that is so cool. " Kaiju's beer was mostly untouched, so he waved off the refill.

"Wait a minute. I'm telling about how I faced down a charging Tortantula on Sevalax wearing only my CASPer longjohns and a belt knife..." Ginzberg tried to regain the floor.

"But, pinplants!" Kaiju interrupted. "Man, you've got to have 'plants if you want to drive the Mark Nines. After I finish my first contract term, I've got an option for 'plants. What's it like?"

"Pure hell if you ask me." Jackson said.

"Um, wow! You have 'plants, too? Geez, who *are* you guys?"

Angus looked up from his whisky and muttered. "Feather dusters. No one of any consequence."

"Who am I?" blustered Ginzberg. "The one telling this story, that's who! Now, I was saying, no shit, there I was, on Tic'k!t'ock, squaring off alone against the Zuul when my godforsaken pinplant lost contact..."

"Um, I thought it was Orkutt and the Oogar were charging you..."

Jackson leaned over, and with a slightly tipsy slur said, "Ignore him, kid, that story changes every time. Next thing you know he'll be saying it was a school of Selroth, and all he was wearing was a Speedo and a breath mask."

Ginzberg spat out his beer and started to raise a fist at Jackson. Angus just held out a hand, palm down, between them, and the pair sat back down.

Once the beer was again refilled, Kaiju picked up right where he'd left off. "So, what was it like? Getting pinplants?" He turned to Jackson. "Which number were you?"

Jackson sighed. "Number T00B2. Eleven grunts after Slick, and we all had to sit and listen to him screaming about tentacles..."

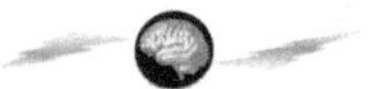

It was not a good section for humans to roam in groups of less than ...oh, company size-. Frankly, no station that catered to mercs was necessarily a 'nice' place to visit, but this district was giving Ginzberg the creeps. He'd survived Jakarta, Detroit, and Pr!lax IV, but he'd never felt the sheer sense of unease as he had the moment he set foot in the To'Os.

It wasn't that this place seemed particularly dangerous, it was more of a sense of uncaring. High on Flake? No one cared. Overcharged at the Bar? Not their concern. Mugged by a G'nish? Too bad, Human, you shouldn't have come alone.

The thing was, he wasn't alone, he had a whole squad of Riedel's Rächer with him (including Jackson, his friend since boot) but it didn't seem to matter. People entering the To'Os had been known to disappear, and there was a rumor that at least one merc company had never been heard of after daring the To'Os.

"The KAS isn't working, I can't pull up a map of this area," one of his squadmates said. The Kartenausschnitt, or KAS, was equal parts GPS, inertial navigation, blue-force tracker and infogrid terminal. If the KAS couldn't map an area, it didn't exist, or someone wanted to make sure that it couldn't be found.

"That's because the Tossers don't want anyone wandering in here, map or not," Jackson told the soldier. "It doesn't matter. The place we want is down this street, left into the alley and then halfway down on the right."

"You've been here before." Oberstabsgefreiter Beitel didn't phrase it as a question.

"We both have," answered Ginzberg. "Didn't like it then, don't like it now, but when Oberst Riedel inquired about equipping us with pinplants, he was referred to this place."

"If you've already got your 'plants, why are you here now?" That was Schmidt, the gefreiter—private—who'd been fiddling with the KAS. He still acted like a raw boot recruit, even though he'd come on for the latter half of the Pr!lax campaign. He still hadn't learned to keep his mouth shut and listen to his sergeants—Feldwebel in the official German rank structure used by the Rächer. Beitel just smacked him in the back of the head, her armored gauntlet ringing off of his helmet.

"Scheisskopf. We were here for pre-op. They don't see too many humans in To'Os, so Squiddy needed morphometric data. He's done a few since then, and they've all worked fine, so the Colonel sent *us* to make sure you lot get 'planted safely."

What was left unsaid was that they were all expendable. Riedel's Rächer—Revengers in English—needed NCOs and officers with the implanted bio-machine links to be able to compete with the offworld merc companies. Before Oberst Gernot Riedel dared risk his officers, he sent Ginzberg's squad to go first. It wasn't that they were worthless guinea pigs, after all, Ginzberg and Jackson were NCO's with not just training, but experience in Earth and Galactic campaigns. Beitel was likely to be heading up the training cadre once she got a bit more rank and seasoning, and the privates would become Headquarters specialists running computers, communications and logistics. It was more that since these troops weren't in the direct command structure now, the Company could afford the personnel shortage and recuperation time needed to recover from surgery and training.

There was one last unspoken detail: If the implants were successful. That had been the reason for Ginzberg and Jackson's preliminary visit, but this was the real thing. Riedel had arranged for a discrete human clinic on W-K Station to study the soldiers after they were released, just in case of complications. The fact that they were interested in duplicating the implants in the future was just a bonus.

The party turned down the alley, and immediately lost the scant overhead light from the glowstrips overhead. The indirect light left shadows everywhere, and many of those shadows moved. Jackson had been leading, since he had better position sense than most (and was usually assigned as guide to the Leutnants who were forever getting lost on field exercises). He stopped and turned, holding up a clenched fist to instruct the rest of the party to freeze, but it was too late to dodge the object that had been tossed at his head.

With their point man down, Ginzberg tapped Beitel on the shoulder and motioned for her to guard the rear. He then moved up to the front and checked the surrounding area before checking Jackson. The latter was moving, albeit slowly, so Ginzberg kept looking around to find the attacker. He'd bent at the knees and kept his back straight so that he could spring into action if necessary. Very slowly, he reached up to the side of his helmet and touched the switch that deployed his night vision goggles. The greenish lighting in his NVGs wasn't much better than the indirect lighting of the alley. There were heat sources all around. Most were cooler than the bodies of his human companions, but that didn't mean much in a Galactic Society with thousands of races ranging from cold-to-hot blooded, and insectoid to giant slime molds.

The sergeant held up his hand and the squad froze. He was facing at a right angle to the rest of the part, staring at a particularly dark pocket of shadow. He was perfectly still for long moments, then burst out from his squatting position and dove into the shadow, coming up with a small struggling creature. Ginzberg's quarry was struggling, biting, and howling, but his held it firmly with both hands clasped around the neck. One hand of the creature held a piece of brick similar to the one on the ground near Jackson.

Now that the other Sergeant was up, he reached for his belt and pulled up powerful flashlight. He shined it on the creature in Ginzberg's grip, revealing an immature dog or wolf-like creature with a mouth full of sharp teeth. It kept trying to bite its captor, but Ginzberg held it at arm's length, and the teeth were unable to reach him. Likewise, the pup kept trying to swing the brick at him, but its arms were too short to be effective.

"Besquith" Jackson said. "Juvenile, which is good for us. What are you going to do with it?"

"Grab the med kit." Ginzberg grunted, dodging the brick that the pup had finally decide to throw at the man who held it by the throat. "'Bes-kit's' can be knocked out with some of our stronger pain killers. Get a fentanyl stick...um..." He bounced the pup up and down a few times to estimate its weight. "Twenty kilos, give or take. Five milligrams should do it."

"Where? He won't stay still!"

While the other sergeant readied the injection, Ginzberg carefully shifted his grip. "Back of the neck, right below my hand. ...and if you value your life, do NOT stick me with that thing!"

It took a few moments, both to get the autosyringe in position, and for the pup to stop moving after the injection. The rest of the squad stayed alert, but nothing else came out of the darkness at them. Jackson flashed his light back into the shadowy area where the pup had been hiding, revealing a sleeping nest, empty food packs and a pile of bricks. He pushed at the nest with his foot, uncovered a pile of material that glittered in the light.

"Gutter rat" Ginzberg pronounced as he laid the pup back on its nest. "Come on, we're going to be late."

"You're just leaving him here?" asked one of the privates.

"It's where he lives," supplied Beitel, then slapped the private on the back of the head. "Feldwebel said move it."

The sign on the door was marked in alien script. They'd had no other encounters during the short trip down the alley. Ginzberg called a halt, directed the squad to check the perimeter, then nodded to Jackson to open the door. Beitel did a clearance entry, hugging the doorframe with her sidearm held at low-ready, with Jackson right on her tail.

A synthesized voice boomed through the doorway from inside. "Damned mercs, always doing a combat entry! I run a clean establishment!"

Jackson's voice answered in return: "It's nice to see you, too, Squiddy, but we got ambushed in the alley."

"One wolf cub hardly counts as an ambush, Human!"

Ginzberg had motioned to the rest of the squad, following them through the door into the clinic. "You were watching? Why didn't you do anything?"

"What was I to do, Human? I am a humble surgeon, not a big strong mercenary like you!" The voice came from a series of small speakers around the room, and from the conveyance of what appeared to be a four-foot octopus. It sat on what looked for all the world like a tall bar stool with motorized wheels. The "seat" of the chair was roughly cup-shaped, and held the body of the creature plus a small amount of water. There were several articulated "arms" sticking out from the chair, holding various medical devices and scanners, and a control console with multiple screens directly in front of the cephalopod's single eye. Its tentacles were draped over the various instruments and arms. They were in constant motion, reminding Ginzberg of snakes. They moved with purpose, however, constantly adjusting and controlling the chair's attachments.

"You're a menace, that's what you are, Squiddy. Anyone that knows you would be afraid of you if they knew you were entering the fight." Ginzberg's voice was light, and it was clearly meant to be a jest, but the members of the squad could tell that there was a grain of truthfulness in the statements as well. "Well, I suppose I should introduce your victims. You remember Jackson, right?"

"We Wrogul never forget, human. It is good to see you again, Sergeant Jackson."

"Corporal Beitel, Private First Class Giorgios and Privates Markos and Lomidze. Markos is the one with the dents in his helmet from getting smacked in the back of his head for asking dumb questions. PFC Giorgios is the one with his back against the door shaking. Giorgios, I know you tested low in xenophobia, what's your malfunction?"

"S-sn-snakes. I h-hate sn-snakes, s- s- sir!"

"Oh, hell. I'll overlook that slur on my parentage for now. How the hell did you end up in an expeditionary force with a fear of snakes?" Ginzberg was frustrated. Given the species a merc was likely to encounter, fear of other species was usually weeded out. Rage, anger, aggression...those were acceptable, but fear usually drummed a recruit out of boot.

"N- never c- came up, s- si- Sergeant!"

Ginzberg noticed Jackson going for the medkit, and gave a slight nod. They didn't need this right now.

"If it makes you feel better," The Wrogul's voice boomed throughout the room, "they are *tentacles*, Private First Class Giorgios. I understand my kind are *very* popular in your Japanese film industry."

Beitel gulped and turned red.

"As physicians!" The Wrogul's voice came from all speakers, as before, but then switched to only the speaker closest to the junior NCO. "Why? What did you have in mind Corporal?"

If anything, Beitel turned even redder. Markos laughed and Jackson started coughing from trying to hold in the laughter.

"Excuse me a moment, Squiddy." Ginzberg interrupted. "Obergefreiter Giorgios! Beachtung!"

The soldier snapped to attention, eyes forward; allowing Jackson to slip in out of his field of view and apply the autojector. The PFC held at attention for a moment, then relaxed. He didn't quite collapse, but his eyes fluttered closed and his chin settled into his chest. After about 30 seconds, his eyes opened and he straightened out. "Thanks," he mumbled.

"Hmph. Val-Z?" Ginzberg asked Jackson. The latter just nodded, acknowledging that he'd only delivered an anti-anxiety drug and not a sedative. "Good. I wouldn't want to have to adjust his meds. Right, Squiddy?" He turned back to the surgeon.

"Indeed, Sergeant Ginzberg. You humans are so septic, it's a wonder you don't get terribly sick every time you get punctured. Oh...wait...you *do*!"

Jackson laughed, but Ginzberg just scowled. "Okay, let's get this over with. Who's first?"

"Me," said Beitel. "Just one thing, how does this work? And how are you implanting it?"

They knew the basics, pinplants were in use as an essential brain-to-computer interface throughout many of the Galactic races. Oh, there were some who frowned on it, and others for whom the implant was...problematic. However, as long as a species had a dedicated cognitive ganglion—a brain in human terms—they could be fitted with a pinplant. Earth had experimented with BCIs since the late twentieth century, the earliest being used to restore hearing by placing an electrode into the inner ear and electrically stimulating the cells that connected to the hearing centers of the brain.

In the twenty-first century, BCIs consisting of thumbnail-sized chips with hundreds of fine metallic spikes were placed on the brain areas controlling muscle movement as well as the touch-sensitive brain regions for those same muscle. Rudimentary artificial limbs could be controlled by mental signals alone, and one team actually used a similar technique to boost memory capability, but they'd never become widespread due to the surgery required to place the interfaces into the brain.

Galactic nanotechnology and Wrogul surgical techniques changed all of that. Nanites were injected into the appropriate brain areas and self-assembled into a mesh connecting movement, sensory, language, hearing and vision areas of the brain to an interface 'Pin' placed just behind the recipient's ear. Computers, comm units, exoskeletal suits, even CASPers could be connected via a hard-wired cable. Some species such as the Wrogul built wireless communications directly into the nano-mesh, but the humans would have to settle for attaching a thumb-sized transceiver to the Pin.

Squiddy had explained it during the Sergeants' prior visit: Human brains were complex chemical and electrical machines, but only at very low power. The Wrogul had not yet figured out how to power some of the more advanced pinplant functions without requiring an external power source, although he assured them that he had a colleague who was building a 'model' human brain to try to figure it out. Thus, these pinplants would not be capable of some extreme functions such as cognitive enhancement. Furthermore, certain functions such as memory caching and increased processing speed would only be available when hardwired to an external device capable of providing additional power to the pinplant. Given that the main anticipated uses for mercs were computer interfacing and control of their warmachines, the power requirements were not anticipated to be a problem.

In response to Beitel's question, Squiddy manipulated one of the articulated arms on his chair. One part of the arm was a vial filled with a silvery liquid that sloshed very slowly as it moved. "I will inject these nano-assemblers into certain parts of your brain. The assemblers will build the neural mesh required to connect to the pinplant pedestal." Another arm held up a flat disk with a one-centimeter pin sticking out at right angles. "Then I'll need to figure out where to put the power supply." Several tentacles surrounded a 5-centimeter-diameter sphere and appeared to lift it with difficulty.

Beitel paled, and swallowed audibly. Markos stepped back, and Lomidze gasped.

"I kid, I kid." Squiddy said, tossed the ball easily from tentacle to tentacle. He squeezed it and it squeaked. "I just keep that to tease the humans." He squeezed it several times with different tentacles, sounding like a dog playing with a toy. "It's also good for strength exercises."

Beitel gulped again, and continued in a much more subdued voice. "But, I mean how do you get the nanites into my brain?"

"With these, of course!" Squiddy held up two tentacles. They were slightly different from the others, much smoother and tapered to an extremely fine point. They were no less functional, though, since he was able to curl them all the way up, then extend them all the way straight—at least two feet in length.

There was a thud, and the squad turned in time to see that Giorgios had hit the floor. He'd been tracking better that last couple of minutes, but now he was out cold on the floor. He'd apparently fainted.

"Actually, I think he goes first," said Jackson.

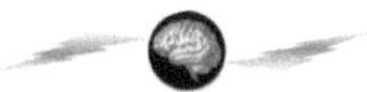

Ginzberg awoke to the sounds of sobbing. He thought it was Giorgios, but it was hard to be sure. After a few moments of listening, he could make out "The tentacles, the tentacles..." Yes, that was Giorgios.

"That's it?" Ginzberg asked.

"Yes, the primary matrix is inserted. It will take several days for the mesh to fully develop." Squiddy's voice came from a speaker somewhere to the left of the couch Ginzberg was reclining on.

"What about the others?"

"While we speak, I am finishing up with Corporal Beitel and starting Sergeant Jackson." The voice now came from two different speakers off to the right. Ginzberg turned his head and could see instruments moving above the two closest couches. Three more couches were occupied, including the moaning Giorgios. "I do not understand why you humans will not allow me to develop a full-cognitive integration system. Multi-tasking is okay, but full hyperthreading is better."

Having developed the pinplant technology to its current state of the art, Wrogul had taken it to an extreme of fully integrating computer technology into their brains. Mercs were being pinned to better function on the battlefield, but didn't quite trust the idea of merging with a computer and letting it make battlefield decisions.

"I know the power supply is a problem," Squiddy continued, "But I can make a device that can be carried externally. After all! Your human males carry very important reproductive databases externally! What's one more 'appendage?'" The voice returned to the speaker on his left. "There I have finished with your Privates." Ginzberg instinctively lowered his hands to the vicinity of the aforementioned 'reproductive database' and flinched.

Scratchy laughter filled the room from all speakers: "Ha! You humans, so gullible! No, I meant that I have finished with Markos and Lomidze. Beitel should start waking up, now, and Jackson should be another twenty of your minutes.

Ginzberg lay back and closed his eyes. He only knew one Wrogul, so he had no idea if the rest of the alien race shared Squiddy's crude humor. He had to admit, it was somewhat appropriate for a seedy clinic catering to mercs. The humor would not be out of place in any combat surgical hospital. It was just...bizarre...hearing it from an intelligent octopus that had just had its tentacles up various...orifices.

Giorgios might be right. Best not to think that way.

"So...how do we ...know if the ...pinplants ... are working?" That was Beitel, speaking slowly as the effects of the surgical field wore off.

"They are currently blocked until I release them." Squiddy spoke over the room speakers. He was currently located at the head of Jackson's couch, and appeared to be fully...immersed...in that procedure while still carrying on the conversation. "The mesh will not be fully mature for several days, but you should be able to access basic functions in a few hours...once I release the blocks of course. Since your Kommandant Riedel would not allow me to include integrated power supplies..."

Ginzberg could have *sworn* he heard the words 'wink, wink, nudge, nudge' come from the speaker beside his head.

Squiddy's voice continued: "...I have applied an auxiliary power module to your pin." All of the soldiers that were currently awake could be seen raising their hands to a point behind their right ear, where they encountered a device covering the pin that extended up over their ear like a hearing aid. "It's supplying power for the nanoassemblers building your mesh, and will function as your wireless interface once I unlock the function links. For now, you should *rest* and I will show you how to access your plants when you wake up."

There was a strange resonance as Ginzberg word the word 'rest.' The voice had come from all speakers, and seemed to reverberate through the room. He also felt very sleepy all of a sudden. Was this another function of the pin-

When Ginzberg awoke the second time, all of the medical instrumentation was gone, and Squiddy was nowhere to be seen. What *was* present was an apparent voice in his head droning on something about ...let's see...".…command syntax for the model H-stroke-alpha mark-three pinplant. Commands may be thought or spoken. Guild authority recommends that users practice command syntax in the spoken form before attempting non-verbal commands. Please note that all verbal pin commands must be preceded by the activation code-phrase 'pin command.' Commands are as follows: 1 of 492, 'Able' The Able verb command activates the option subset for subsequent verb activation commands. Options from the Able command can be used to modify…" He shifted his attention to the rest of the room, and the voice seemed to fade into the background.

The rest of his squad was sitting up from their couches. Some looked confused, like Beitel, others looked distracted, like Jackson. Giorgios had a wild look in his eyes; the 'voices in his head' might prove to be a problem.

"Squiddy?" Ginzberg asked, but there was no immediate response.

"Are we done?" asked Lomidze, in his near incomprehensible Georgian (the country, not the state) accent.

"Yes, my friends, you are done." Squiddy's voice came from all of the speakers, back to the booming sound they'd encountered when they first entered the clinic. "I was just reviewing the results of your PET scans. The sleep command was a very specific test of the feedback interface. The appropriate brain areas responded exactly the way they were meant to. You may go on your way."

"Good," said Ginzberg, standing up. "We need to get back to base."

"Wait," said Jackson, almost simultaneously . "Let's not forget that we left an angry, tranquilized Besquith pup out there. Perhaps we need to recover a bit more so that we're not distracted…"

"Um, did you say pet scan? As in dogs and cats type of pets?" asked Markos. Beitel reached over and slapped him on the back of the head.

"No, Private Markos, PET scan as in Positron Emission Tomography. It's an imaging technique to see what part of your brain is metabolically active following a stimulus. I stimulated your pinplants, and watched to see which brain areas were active. It's a standard procedure that even humans apply. To their dogs and cats, even!" Squiddy's speakers produced his near laugh again.

"Wait...positron emission..." Beitel's face screwed up in a grimace. "YOU INJECTED ANTIMATTER INTO MY BRAIN?" She began looking around for something to punch, was about to settle for punching Markos, when Jackson held out a hand and restrained her.

"Well, technically, no. I injected a radioisotope of fluorine into your brain. When the isotope breaks down and emits positrons, the scanner records where that occurred. If it makes you feel better, your brain produced the antimatter!"

"THAT'S NOT ANY BETTER!" shouted Beitel. Jackson moved to intercept her as she moved away, and contemplated restraining her with both hands.

"...and the fluorine-18 produces gamma rays as well!"

"Not helping!" shouted Jackson as Beitel just screamed in rage.

"Perhaps it is time for you to go." A door opened in the blank wall, and they could see the alley outside the clinic. "Perhaps I turned up the aggressive/alert functions a bit much when I tried to give you a competitive edge over that poor little puppy dog. The furniture sank into the floor and the back wall started moving to force them outside. As the door closed behind them, they heard: "Good-bye! Have a nice day! Remember to refer all of your friends to Squiddy's!"

The trip back to the docks and their transport was uneventful...if one considered subduing a pack of 5 adult Besquith backing up the gutter-rat pup they'd encountered earlier...a brawl with a dozen human mercs that came spilling out of a bar wrestling an inebriated Oogar as the squad was passing...and the platoon of Lumar security goons that the bartender called in to escort the whole lot either to the brig or their ships.

Perhaps Squiddy *had* set the pinplants to stimulate the aggression centers a bit too much.

It was late and the bar was emptying out. Jackson was staring into his beer. Kaiju was at the bar arguing with the bartender about his not-inconsiderable tab. Angus had fallen asleep several times, and had been helped back to his quarters by a couple of patrons wearing a uniform similar to the inebriated Scot. Only the old soldier with the DFT remained at the bar. Rumor had it he lived in a back room. Having a DFT meant that a powerful race of near mystical assassins owed him a favor. It also made him a target. Ginzberg had never seen the man enter or leave. He was just...there.

They sat without talking for a while.

The problem with 'plant assisted memory was that when you called it up, you got *everything* right down to the smell of the battlefield. The 'plants had gotten better over the years, and he'd made many return visits to Squiddy for upgrades. They'd finally fixed the power requirements, and Ginzberg's last upgrade had given him the full memory-caching capability.

It wasn't without price, he thought as he continued to ruminate in silence.

He remembered so clearly how it had felt when the pinplants came fully online a week or so after the surgery. All of his senses were alive with the ability to amplify and enhance at will. The first time he'd plugged into a battlefield information system, he'd felt like a god. The ability to see everything in one glance, to know without doubt where his squadmates were located. For a time, it seemed like it was the ultimate advantage.

That memory triggered another—associative memory cascades were a bitch for a pinned soldier who'd gotten too deep into his wine. The first time he'd gotten into a 'plant-capable CASPer. He didn't just *wear* the warmachine, he *was* the warmachine, and all of the excitement and power and elation came flooding back, lifting his spirits, even if temporarily. But then there was the time they come back from a deployment and found Colonel Riedel dead by his own hand. He'd pinned into the administrative 'net, started sorting through the comm traffic of the last few days and discovered that the Company was bankrupt. He was going to have to explain to the troops that the Rächer were disbanded and couldn't payout what they were owed.

The good and the bad, the beautiful and the ugly. You only got out of the 'plants what you put into them. The thought turned Ginzberg's attention back to Kaiju. It was hard to believe that he and Jackson had been that new, that...*shiny*...once. He looked over at Jackson. "Do you think he bought it?"

"I doubt it. You and I know it, and he's been in long enough to know full well they don't serial number the 'plants. At least, not in standard."

"I thought your line about '...listening to him screaming about tentacles...' was inspired. I especially liked how you acted it out. You looked just like that PFC, what was his name?"

"Giorgios. Bought it on Orkutt."

"Oh, yeah. Somehow, I should have remembered that."

Jackson just gave him a look of disbelief. "Markos is a businessman; can you believe it? Import/export out of Piquaw. Lomidze went officer. Was trying for that Swiss outfit."

"Beitel."

"Yeah. Damn shame. She would have made a good sergeant."

"Right. One person. ONE PERSON in our company gets the allergic reaction to nanites and it's Beitel." Ginzberg raised his almost empty glass. "Absent companions."

Jackson nodded agreement, then drained the last of his beer. He stopped, and a wry grin appeared on his face. "Do you think they still employ that Jeha scanner mech tech at Peepo's?"

Ginzberg smiled in return. "Yeah. They do. I had to get a scan last month." His grin grew larger. "Why, are you thinking what I'm thinking?"

Jackson's grin matched Ginzberg's. "Oh yeah. I mean, can you imagine the kid's face when he's being prepped for his pre-pinplant scans and in walks a six-foot centipede in coveralls, carrying a toolbox?"

EARWORM

Authors note: No sooner had Headspace and Timing appeared in print but I knew I needed to continue the story. Here then are Squiddy, Jackson, and Ginzberg, a few years later...

"...and there was Giorgios, muttering 'the tentacles, the tentacles.'"

"You're not telling it right, Kaiju." Jackson whispered in the ear of the Obertstabsgefreiter—Corporal in the English-speaking units. "You have to lower your voice when Squiddy asks Beitel 'Why, what did you have in mind, my dear?'"

Kaiju turned to his senior NCO and whispered back. "Sorry Hauptfeldwebel Jackson, I know Ginzberg tells it so much better, but I couldn't resist." Kaiju turned back to the pair of wide-eyed Gefreiter—buck privates with no combat experience—and resumed a livelier retelling of tale that he'd heard back when he was their age and rank. "There I was, standing up naked two klicks behind enemy lines with nothing but my haptic suit on..."

"You know the difference between a fairy tale and a war story?" said a voice in Jackson's own ear.

"Sure, the fairy tale starts 'Once upon a time,' the war story starts 'No shit, there I was.'" Jackson turned to see a short woman with close-cropped black hair. "Katie. What brings you down out of orbit? I thought you were going to sign on with the Hussars? Sit. Let me get you a drink." Turning back to the table, he interrupted the corporal's story and introduced his friend. "Guys, let me introduce Kathryn T. 'Katie' Andalusia, the best pilot ever to land a dropship in a hot LZ."

Once the introductions were complete, Jackson motioned to the bartender then turned back to the pilot. "So? What about the Hussars?"

Katie sighed. "I need to get another set of 'pins.'" She brushed the short hair enough to reveal the pin-like computer linkage behind her ear. "Apparently the Hussars are taking a cue from the Golden Horde and starting to require dual pinplants for critical operators."

"What? Why? How many?"

"Well, rumor has it that several of the leaders of the Horsemen have multiple pinplants—more than two, even—but the Hussars just need me to get a second set. For now." The serverbot had delivered a round of drinks for the table. Katie took her beer, and drained half of the glass in one motion. "Anyway, I heard about Ginzberg and thought I'd drop in to see how you were holding up."

"I can't say it's been easy. We lost a lot of good troops when the Rächer dissolved. We kicked around a bit until I heard that someone picked up Riedel's old charter. 'Polonius's Rächer' doesn't have the same ring, but we managed to get a few NCOs back and have trained up some cadre to fill in the TOE. Kaiju's a corporal already and will eventually make a good sergeant and even Top, but I'm not too thrilled about moving up."

Katie raised an eyebrow.

"Yeah, Oberst Polo wants me for sergeant-major. I'm happier just making sure the good ell-tees keep their heads down." He paused and looked over at the bar, then started to rise from his seat. "Speaking of, excuse me..."

The newcomer at the bar was in brand new, neatly pressed ACUs, with Leutnant—Second Lieutenant—pips and the Rächer unit patch. He had his hand raised, a shiny coin in it. Before the coin could strike the bar-top, the bartenders hand lashed out and enclosed both the coin and the lieutenant's hand in a tight grip. The bartender didn't speak, just stood there, stone-faced while Jackson hurried up.

"Sir. You really don't want to do that in here." Jackson turned to the bartender and nodded. "Thanks, G, I've got this."

The officer pulled his hand back and drew himself up to stare at the sergeant. The fact that he was a fresh-faced kid trying to stare down a grizzled veteran slowly dawned on him and he slumped back down and put his coin back in his pocket.

"This is another one of those 'Old Sarge, Young Ell-tee' moments again, isn't it?" The kid asked.

"It can be." Jackson led him to a chair at the empty table next to his own. That way the officer was not obviously sitting with the enlisted, but was near enough to be watched by his senior NCO. "Look, Lieutenant, if you want to buy a drink for yourself, or even a buddy, there's cheaper ways to do it than by losing a coin challenge and buying the house the next round...that is, unless you *want* to buy the house a round. I guarantee you that everyone in this place has his coin, and most of them are older and higher ranked than yours. Save your money and keep your coin until it looks like this." Jackson flashed his coin with the German eagle on one face. It was old, and some of the ridges on the edge were worn down. It appeared to have been nicked by an energy beam at one time. Jackson leaned closer and lowered his voice, "and let me take yours down to the CASPer shop and put a little wear and tear on it so that it's not so obviously new."

He got the lieutenant set up with a drink and turned back to Katie. She was staring at the bartender. It was the first she had noticed the man standing there, serving drinks without talking or changing expression. "What exactly happened to him?"

"He doesn't remember. The Colonel had promoted him to sergeant major, and was sending him for additional 'pins. It seems everyone else wants to emulate the Horde, too." Jackson drained his beer and checked with the others at the table. He looked around the bar, noticed a couple of new groups had come in and saw a few obvious newbies—they were probably flush with signing bonuses. He grinned a sly grin and turned to wink at Katie. He flipped his coin in the air and the sound of metal hitting the table silenced the room. There was a flurry of hands reaching for pockets, and sure enough one of the new privates came up short. His group glared back at Jackson, but the older mercs all grinned.

Jackson leaned back to whisper to the junior officer. "See, sir? It's a matter of timing, and knowing the room."

Once the new round of drinks arrived, Jackson continued the conversation with Katie. "The only thing the unit knows is that Ginzberg went off to see Squiddy for *his* second set of 'plants. We had just come off of our first mission with me as Top and 'G' as smaj. It was *supposed* to be a smash-and-grab on a suspected Kahramann lab, but apparently someone else had the same idea. There were at least two more merc units in the field and we *think* there was a third besides us, but we never actually saw them." Jackson took another pull from his glass and then stared into it for a moment before continuing. "Anyway, we got home mostly intact, but the battlespace nearly got away from us. Oberst Polo had the bright idea that Ginzberg needed more pins to handle the data flow, so he sent him off to see Squiddy. The process shouldn't have taken more than a day, plus the usual week in transit each way. Three weeks passed and we didn't hear from him. After a month we sent someone to Squiddy's. Gone, cleaned out. Station records showed the Sergeant Major arriving, but never leaving. Another month and we wrote him off as MIA, then we got a tip relayed on a courier from an 'anonymous source.' It let us track his pins, and we found him back on To'Os in the middle of an absolute cluster-fuck." Jackson gestured to the bartender who was cleaning glasses with almost automaton-like movements. He turned to place the glasses behind the bar, and for the first time they could see the left side of his head. Above the left ear was a rectangle where the skin had been replaced by a grid that looked almost like multiple pinplants, but the whole assembly sparkled with internal light. "The doc who treated him says those are advanced pinlinks, similar to what the Wrogul use on themselves. He also said that the human brain was not meant for that level of digital communication."

"So, what...who did this?" Katie asked.

"We don't know all of the story. A Peacemaker got involved, and Oberst Polo says a lot of it needs to stay under seal for the investigation. Whatever it was, it broke him. He does what he's told, and just hums to himself all the time. The owner gave him a job since we're always in here between assignments. We can all keep an eye on him and watch for any long-term side effects."

"What if he's a deep sleeper agent?" Katie mused. "Or a spy?"

"This is a grunt bar, and we're armed mercs," Jackson answered. "Besides, there's a dampener in the bar. He wouldn't be transmitting more than a meter, and a technical team from the Rächer run a sweep of the bar and his quarters upstairs every day."

"Then what? He just tends bar? Look at him, he might as well be a robot."

"The Colonel conferred with the leaders of the Four Horsemen. Apparently they have a plan, and we're just supposed to watch 'G' for a while. It's above my paygrade."

"You say he's humming?"

"Yeah, under his breath most of the time. Every once in a while it's audible, and I even heard him whistle once. Always the same tune, sounds familiar, too. Like something I heard in childhood."

The bartender began to mutter under his breath. "Dah-di-dah-dum, dah-dee-dum." His voice raised slightly in pitch. "Daah-di-dah-dum, daah-dee-dum." Once more he raised the pitch. "Daaah-di-dah-dum, daaah-dee-dum. Da-dee-daaaah-daaaaah-dum."

Ginzberg lost count of the times hid been to Squiddy's clinic in the back-alleys of To'Os. As more human mercenaries opted for the brain-to-computer interfacing pinplants, there had been talk about moving Squiddy to a more 'human-friendly' environment. The problem with that was that Squiddy really didn't want to move. He relished the image of a back-alley, 'less-than-reputable' 'Plant Palace, and really didn't want the attention he would incur to throw his fortunes in with the Union's newest mercs. The mercs accepted it as status quo, and simply did a bit of 'clean-up' to ensure that 'plant patients could get from port to clinic without running afoul of too many gutter-rats.

He smiled as he remembered bring his squad in for their first pinning. There was the corner where the Besquith gutter-rat had made his nest. That corner was where, afterward the implant, Beitel had decided she could take down two adult Besquith single handedly. Her aggression center had been stimulated a bit too much during pinning, so it was fortunate that there hadn't been any Besquith present, or she would never have survived the encounter without her CASPer. Squiddy's door was just ahead, and a subtle indicator light said the clinic was available for hire.

"First Sergeant Ginzberg. Welcome!" Squiddy's voice came from several speakers around the room. In the absence of other customers, he had the volume set quite loud, and the effect was similar to shouting. "Easy Squiddy, my hearing is not going bad...yet. Besides, it's Hauptfeldwebel, now. Sergeant Major."

"Of course, of course. You mercs are always changing ranks." Squiddy came out from behind several pieces of equipment in his usual four-foot-tall rolling chair with the cup-shaped seat half filled with water. The octopoid Wrogul's arms were always in motion, leading one of Ginzberg's earliest troops to mistake them for snakes. "What? Alone? Why have you not brought me fresh victims? Do you not trust me with your Privates? <sngh, sngh, sngh>" The scratchy sound coming from the speakers was the Wrogul equivalent of laughter. Ginzberg didn't know if it was typical of the aliens, but Squiddy was quite fond of jokes, the more risqué, the better.

"Not this time, Squiddy. You've become just a bit *too* famous in the Company. There's usually a pool going to see who faints first, or whether the females are going to try to file harassment charges. It's become something of a rite of passage. The sensitive and easily offended don't last long." Ginzberg slung his go bag at a nearby couch and sat down on the one closest to the surgeon. "Nope, just me. The Kommandant says I need a second set of pins."

"Indeed, you are to be battlefield commander? Perhaps your Oberst Riedel wants me to remake you into...what do they call it? 'Red Diamond Man?'"

"Since when do you watch ancient Earth Tri-V, Squiddy?" The entertainment had been popular soon after First Contact, when the people of Earth had been enamored with Galactic Union technology and culture. The show depicted a human astronaut that had been brought back from near-death by Union medicine and technology. The fact that it would have cost more than Earth's entire monetary worth was given only a passing acknowledgement by the title reference to the Union's most valuable trade good. Of course, that was before the Alpha Contracts and the reality of Earth's lowly place in the Union had set in. "No thanks. There's going to be enough computer in my head without turning me into a cyborg."

"Not just in your head, Sergeant Major Ginzberg. As you now know, the first implants you received were not really full pinplants. I knew much about your human brains, but not enough for the full interface. Your first pins connected to motor, visual and auditory cortex to give you the equivalent of computer input 'muscles' and the ability to 'read' and 'hear' computer output. Your human scientist Sato and my Wrogul colleague 'Nemo' figured out most of the interface. Once you survived your first 'plants, you could be upgraded to full interfaces with co-processing, motor planning, intention and decision-making. That set was sufficient for CASPer or spacecraft operation, or just being a really good clerk by augmenting your pre-motor and frontal decision cortices. The co-processor also effectively doubles your computation and communication speed." Squiddy's tentacles took on purposeful movement as he began to adjust the equipment behind the surgical couch. "This second set of pinplants will more extensively target the temporal lobe memory areas, parietal and frontal links to speech and language centers, and quadruple the co-processor capabilities. If you want the full 'Horseman' package you'll get almost eight times the communication speed, and the co-processor will accelerate your brain processes so much that your natural body will seem terribly slow in comparison. We include transmission dampeners in the brainstem and spinal cord to keep you from tearing your muscles apart."

"Umm, no thanks. Just the standard package for a second pair of pins. Superhuman is what I drive a CASPer for."

"Are you sure? Two for one sale today for bilaterally symmetric sophonts! Two arms, two legs, nice tentacles like mine for the ladies? <sngh, sngh, sngh>" The Wrogul held up the specialized appendages he utilized for the surgery.

"You're incorrigible, Squiddy!"

"That's the problem with you humans, no courage for finer things in life!" Squiddy slapped the back of the couch with a wet sound. "It is just as well. Your human brains are so delicate, very few can handle a third or even fourth set of pinplants. It takes a very unusual mind to handle the degree of cybernetics we Wrogul take for granted, it usually drives humans insane."

"What about the Horsemen?" Ginzberg had also heard rumors that several of the Four Horseman mercenary companies required their soldiers to have multiple pinplants. The whispered tales also said that one of the leaders had as many as four pairs of 'plants.

"Ah, well, it is rare even for them, and it is arguable as to whether they are truly sane...at least by human standards. Even the exoskeletal sophonts with their distributed cognitive ganglia can be upgraded more than you poor primates. " He held up the two finer appendages that he used for implanting the nanomachines that built the neural implants. "Lie back, let me get to work. The sooner you are done, the sooner I can get back to watching anime! I love those girls in uniforms."

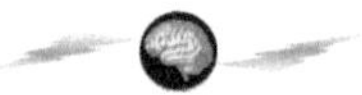

"Sergeant Major. Ginzberg. Wake up. You must get moving."

Ginzberg opened his eyes. He was no longer in Squiddy's clinic—at least not a part he had seen before. The ceiling was low, and the room was dark, just a flickering light in the distance. "Uh...Wha?'"

"Hauptfeldwebel Ginzberg. You must wake up. You are in danger."

"Wait...what? Are we done? "

"You are done. You must leave. I have hidden you in my storage room, but there are MinSha in the outer clinic. You are in danger if they find you."

"Uh..." Ginzberg's head still wasn't clear, and just like the other times he'd been pinplanted, it felt like there was a voice running in the back of his brain, providing a running commentary on his new capabilities.

"Co-processor One on-line. Co-processor Two, integration Twenty-five percent complete. Co-processor Two will be on-line in twelve minutes. Sensory monitors on-line, room temperature is sixteen degrees Celsius, illumination forty percent of Sol normal, gravity zero-point nine Earth normal, oxygen one hundred 10 percent of Earth normal. There is an auditory alarm, temperature is rising and there are combustion residues in the air..."

The damn 'plants were giving a boot-up report!

"...Motor Integration Processor One is on-line. MIP Two integration is thirty-five percent. Reaction time augmentation is at one-hundred seventy-five percent and increasing..." *<First Sergeant Ginzberg, you must exit NOW!>* That last was not in the computer voice he associated with the pinplant orientation.

"Squiddy? Why are you in my head?"

<Ginzberg, get moving now. The clinic was attacked, I had to leave. Your pins are complete and I've shielded you from their systems for now.> He wasn't on one of the clinic bio-beds, but rather a low table in what looked like a storage room. He could hear a scratching and thudding sound behind the nearest wall.

Right. Storage room. Squiddy's gone, and there's enemy on the other side of the wall—looking for him.

Why were they looking for him?

Ginzberg wasn't a Horseman, he wasn't a Merc Commander, he was just an NCO from a mid-sized merc company fighting its way back from near bankruptcy. He was a worthless hostage and a lousy source of intel. Why were they after him?

More scratching. Chittering.

MinSha.

Damned bugs. Ginzberg's family was Jewish, not Iranian, but you didn't have to be of Persian descent to hold a grudge against the race that had glassed a large portion of the Middle East. Spurred by a mixture of fear and hatred, he finally sat up and looked around.

Storage room, one each. Plasteel shelves holding plasteel storage containers. Some of the containers were transparent and Ginzberg caught glimpses of things he'd rather forget. *Were those EYES?* As he started to move around the room, he saw a brief flash of light and turned to see what it was. A faint greenish glow seemed to be coming from one wall near floor level. As he moved to investigate, the green light moved until it reached a darkened area. The light ringed the dark patch and pulsed slightly.

A section of wall opened up, and the green glow moved into the opening and appeared to move down, out of view. After a moment, the rim of the opening flashed green again, then the light entered the opening and moved down the tunnel again. When it happened a third time, the flashing seemed to take on a sense of urgency.

"Okay, I get it. Go through here, and do it quickly." He took one last look around the room. He could hear the sound of scratching and hammering at the wall. The MinSha and whoever else were on the other side would soon break through.

Oops. His final glance around the room settled on a small pack on the floor next to the table he woke up on. *My gear, I'm going to need that, and I* really *don't want the bugs to get it.* Grabbing the pack, he ducked into the tunnel. The green light was now rimmed in red, and it was quickly moving a short distance into the tunnel, then back to the entrance and repeating. Ginzberg moved completely into the tunnel as far as the light had traveled, and he could sense the opening sealing behind him as cleared the threshold.

It didn't sound as if the MinSha had breached the wall into the storage room, so they shouldn't have seen the green light. Maybe this would be a clean getaway. He started to move down the tunnel, wondering where it led. The green light was back, and he couldn't sense the urgency this time. It stayed just ahead of his position and preceded him down the tunnel.

<You are correct, it is not as urgent, but you must get down this tunnel, exit unseen, and get away from To'Os.>

"Squiddy, you haven't answered how and why this is happening."

<Second pins have a communicator function. It is simple for a cybernetical-ly-linked sophont like myself to transmit directly to your pinplants. Likewise, the light you see guiding you is directly stimulated onto your visual cortex. There was no light for the MinSha to see. In fact, you're not really seeing right now.>

There was a sensation as if a switch had been thrown, and everything went dark. He muffled a shout of surprise, but quickly realized that he wasn't blind, it was just very dark. A very faint light came from the vicinity of his pack. He opened it to see the telltales on his slate and yack. The switch sensation occurred again, and he could see the tunnel and surroundings clearly.

<I downloaded a navigation program into your 'plants and activated it before you woke up. >

"And where are you?"

<I am long gone. I down loaded this conversation as well. You Humans are predictable.>

"Okay, but why are they after me? You didn't answer that...or program it or whatever."

<Again, you Humans. So full of conceit and self-importance. They are not after you, they are after me. You are just collateral damage and a bit of sport.>

"Crap. Damned aliens." He hurried down the tunnel, he could see a rectangle rimmed in red. It was probably the exit.

Upon carefully checking the exit with a fiber 'scope and exiting the cramped tunnel as quietly as possible, Ginzberg looked around to figure out where he was. Oh, joy. To'Os had gotten better the more the human mercs frequented Squiddy's but this was Old Tosser territory. If a human traveled here, it was best to do so in a full company of mercs.

He started to reach for his KAS—his Kartenausschnitt—mapping module, and quickly realized that the intent to go for a map had triggered an overlay in his pinplants.

Oh, this was going to take some getting used to. Let's see, the port was over there, about two klicks. The courier ship he'd arrived on was in berth 73...except it wasn't.

His pins automatically queried the portmaster system and informed him that the courier had boosted twenty minutes ago.

This was turning out to be a craptastic day.

There was only one other human ship in To'Os. It was registered to some executive protection outfit chartered out of one of the Rim worlds: *Custode Sviss* from San Pietro.

Huh. 'Swiss' guards out of an Italian colony world. Well, they were human according to the Merc Guild charter, so hopefully they could be of assistance if it came down to a last stand.

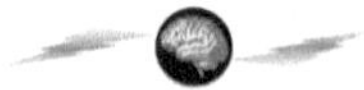

He never made it to the port.

A security patrol picked him up before he'd even gotten a couple of blocks from the tunnel exit. On most ports and stations, security forces were filled by Lumar mercs. The large four-armed humanoids were considered slow and more than a bit dumb by most other races. Ginzberg knew better, Lumari were *simple* which was totally different from being dumb. The aliens did not engage in complicated thinking—when given an objective, they attacked it directly—when told to secure an area, they kept it locked up tight. That same simpleness meant that it was harder to argue your way out of a jam, but they wouldn't be cruel or malicious.

Unfortunately, the patrol was Besquith. Besq's looked like the human notion of werewolves: bipedal with absurdly long arms, muscular wolf features with way too many teeth. They were as cruel as the mythical monsters, too. Ginzberg tried to evade, but knew better than to try to fight the Besquith patrol. It didn't matter; he was beaten and even bitten several times in the course of his 'arrest.'

"Where is T'tch~D!'!'tal?" The questioner was MinSha, a six-foot-tall praying mantis with ruby eyes. All of that race's soldiers were female, but it didn't soften their manner at all.. The very presence of the alien made Ginzberg's skin crawl—not with fear, but anger. She'd pronounced the alien name with a squishing noise in the second syllable and double click in the next to last, but it meant nothing to Ginzberg.

"Who's that?

"I believe you called him 'Squiddy' in your disgusting Human vernacular."

"Nope, can't help you there."

"There is no need," came a new voice. Ginzberg couldn't really turn his head, he was too heavily restrained. He didn't really have peripheral vision, either, given the swelling around his eyes, but the voice was a synthetic, just like the Wrogul surgeon.

Had they caught up with Squiddy? Or had he turned himself in?

Unfortunately, the voice did not belong to the Wrogul with whom Ginzberg was familiar. A water filled tank that looked for all the world like a super-sized Earthside aquarium, rolled up on a motorized carriage. Inside the tank was a mass of arms and tentacles—clearly a Wrogul—but the color seemed off. Instead of a uniform shiny gray, this creature was mottled with black, dark and light gray, and even some white patches that appeared to be loose, decaying skin.

"I thought you said we needed T'tch~D!'!'tal, or preferably the renegade N'mo't!'!'na~tcha?" The MinSha shifted to look at the clearly diseased Wrogul in the tank. "The Boss has not given you much time to produce results."

"There is no need to hunt down the traitors. 'Nemo' hides with his Horseman friends and 'Squiddy' has escaped your feeble attempt, but this disgusting specimen has just been implanted and the nanites are still growing. I can learn much from studying their programming. Who knows, this one might even tell us where to find the traitors!"

"You don't have much time. You promised to deliver the Human-loving Wrogul surgeons, or failing that, to demonstrate that humans could be…What is their word? Oh, yes, 'hacked,' and controlled through their pinplants." The MinSha held up the sharpened blade of her foreleg and made a slashing motion. "Otherwise, we shall find another way of 'hacking' them."

"You will wait" said the Wrogul, moving his tank closer to the chair where Ginzberg was restrained and began to extend arms and tentacles out of the water. "The Boss contracted *me* for this mission. You are simply my escort.

I will produce as promised, I just need to collect a sample." It held up his two manipulatory tentacles.

Unlike Squiddy's smooth, finely tapered tentacles that were able to mysteriously penetrate through skin and bone with no incision or pain, *this* Wrogul's tentacles were coarse and rough. There were bumps and scars, and more than a little reddish discoloration on the surgical appendages.

Fuck. This was going to HURT*!*

Ginzberg did not know how long he'd been out, only that he'd seen the tentacles coming toward him, followed by an indeterminate period of blackness, then a gradual return to consciousness with the sound of screaming in the distance. The more aware he became, the closer the screaming appeared to be, until he realized that it was his own. He felt pressure on the left side of his head, which immediately erupted into pain.

He'd long since stopped screaming, though, which was a relief. His mouth was dry and his throat raw. Not screaming felt better, even though the urge to scream was still present. He briefly considered uttering a curse, but almost as soon as he had the thought, he felt a blinding headache somewhere between his left ear and his temple on that same side.

"Wha?'" he tried, and again felt that sharp pain. "Urgh. Wha's happ'nin?'" he slurred.

"I removed some nanites from your speech and language centers." The synthesized voice of the Wrogul came from somewhere off to the left. Ginzberg had a little peripheral vision on that side, but he couldn't see past a dark, thick liquid that appeared to have dripped down over his left eye. The voice continued. "They were the newest nanites, and I needed them for my study. I left a few of my own design to act as a control link. You will recover. Or not. It means little to me."

"B'st'rd," Ginzberg managed to utter. Every word, every *thought* of speech was painful. The Wrogul laughed that weird hissing and clicking that he'd come to recognize from Squiddy's ribald sense of humor. On *this* Wrogul, it was creepy and sinister.

Much time had passed and he had frequently felt a sensation of worms reaching into his brain—squirming, wriggling, and chewing holes. The very thought made him retch. After a long period of silence, he decided to try speech again. It still gave him a blinding headache, but it took his mind off of the felling of worms. "Do you have...a name?"

"You could not pronounce it, and it be offensive for you to try. I know that Humans like to have convenient names, so you may call me 'Pasteur' for I am about to rid the Union of a terrible plague."

"What...Plague?" It was all he could do to get the words out, but he had to do *something*. To try *anything*!

The Wrogul seemed to ignore him, sitting in its tank doing whatever it was it was doing. He knew it was interacting with the various instruments in the room because it would periodically move the motorized carriage to a new location, and reach an arm or tentacle out to manipulate the strange devices. At some point, Ginzberg's face had been cleaned of dried blood and mucus, and the swelling had gone down enough for his eyes to focus and look about his surroundings. His table had been raised to an angle that let him see, which was how he'd known about the alien's movements. There were no physical restraints, but he was unable to move his body, only his head, which suggested that the restraints were an effect of the new nanites in his body.

"I said. What plague?" It had been an hour since he'd first asked the question.

Mostly the Wrogul stayed away from him, but in response to the repeated question, it moved its tank back to the side of the surgical platform and focused its octopus-like eye at him. The speakers around the room started in with the creepy laughter-equivalent again. Finally, it spoke: "Why, Humans, of course!" It rolled back to its instruments, still laughing.

"In that...case, I...shall call...you...*Mengele*," he gasped with the pain.

The octopoid alien stopped all motion for a moment. In a pinplanted human that usually meant they were using their 'plants to communicate with a computer somewhere. It was probably the same for a cyber-augmented cephalopod. After a moment it 'laughed' again.

"Yes, very interesting. I admire this Doctor Mengele. He had the right ideas." It returned to its work and Ginzberg was treated to a new burst of pain.

There were no references to passing time. Ginzberg knew that time had passed, but there was no way to tell how much. At first it was boredom punctuated by pain, but then the alien he'd dubbed 'Mengele' had started to experiment in earnest. At first all he'd felt was pain, but the alien questioned him about whether he had thoughts or sensations associated with voluntary muscle movements. Soon the pain was accompanied by twitching of arms and legs.

Ginzberg eventually realized that the alien surgeon was trying to reverse engineer the brain-machine interface that allowed a pinned merc to operate a CASPer without a haptic suit. Normally the sensors of the skin-tight garment detected muscle and joint movements and transmitted them to the artificial muscles and joints of the Combat Assault System, Personal. A merc with pinplants could bypass the haptics and directly control the armored combat mecha by *thinking* about moving. Mengele was trying to produce the opposite effect, that is, moving his human limbs via remote control.

The pain was excruciating. From the bruises on his body that he could see with his limited head movement, some of it was physical, but so much more was strictly in his mind. Mengele probed and experimented constantly—there was no day or night. The pain would rise and he would become unconscious. He'd regain consciousness and the pain would start all over again.

He began to see hallucinations. First it was Jackson standing over him, throwing cold water in his face, then it was that girl he met in Kowloon. He was in a bar telling a story to the new kid and watching that kid lose a coin challenge and have to pay for all of the drinks.

The hallucinations talked to him, too. He could see, smell, touch and hear, just like that time his father had taken them all to the theme park in California.

In the back of his mind, he decided Mengele was probing his memories. It wouldn't be enough to control humans like puppets, it would need to control their minds as well.

Ginzberg tried to fight, but it was...Just. So. Damned. Hard.

It was so much easier to simply let go. To take advantage of the mad scientist's manipulations and just live in the memories. He remembered a song. It was something he'd loved when he heard it in the park, but his father had gotten tired of it and yelled at him for singing it all the time.

Something about a small world.

Dah-di-dah-dee-dah-dee-da-da-dee-dum...

There was shouting. Ginzberg didn't pay much attention to the events in the lab. Pain was constant, but at least the twitching had stopped. He was hearing voices now, though. They kept the hallucinations interesting. Dancing dolls, children's voices singing. His father yelling at him to stop singing; his mother telling his father to stop shouting.

He'd never realized how much his father sounded like a Besquith and his mother sounded like a MinSha.

It was a bright and clear Southern California day. There were boats, and they rode the boats into a brightly colored world.

Dee-di-dah-di-dum-dee-di-dee-dum-dum.

"STOP SINGING!" Dad was really mad, now. He was sort of bluish-purple, with red eyes that were really bugging out. He had some sort of knife in each hand, and he was threatening the man who ran the ride. The ride attendant was spilling water out of a fish tank and there was broken glass and blue blood in the water. Meanwhile the lights were all flashing in time with the song.

Da-di-da.   Da-di-da.   Dah-dee-dah.   Dah-dee-dah. *Dah-di-dah-dee-dah-di-dah.*

"We figure Squiddy knew Ginzberg would be caught the moment his new 'plants connected with the Aethernet. G hadn't had them long enough to even realize they'd connect automatically—filtering is a learned skill, and something you have to practice." Jackson drained his beer and raised an eyebrow at Katie. She nodded, and he caught his former NCO's eye and motioned to the pitcher.

"Apparently it wasn't personal, just a delaying tactic. We figured out that Squiddy sent the 'anonymous' tip with the tracking. Oberst Polo still wants to find the slimy bastard." The replacement picture came. The bartender didn't speak or otherwise acknowledge Jackson or Andalusia. "Once we recovered him, the Kommandant sent a message to the Winged Hussars to see if their surgeon, Nemo, could look at him. We never heard back, but one day a Peacemaker shows up with a different Wrogul on tow. "

"Wrogul?" Katie asked. "I didn't know they were Peacemakers."

"Well, every sophont race is supposed to provide members to the Peacemaker Guild. This one wasn't an enforcer, he seemed more like...a Medical Examiner, I guess. The Enforcer was a nasty-tempered Besquith." Jackson shuddered, then looked around to see if anyone appeared to be listening. He lowered his voice and continued. "Anyway, this Wrogul, called himself 'Harryhausen,' checked G over itself. Said it specialized in biotech trouble, and this looked like the work of a rogue calling itself 'Pasteur.' Anyway, Oberst Polo had me assisting the Wrogul, and the moment he ran a diagnostic on G's pins, they dumped a huge record file. There's a whole lot of processing and memory crammed in Ginzberg's head, now, and so far there's no way of knowing how much was from Squiddy, and how much from the 'Pasteur' bastard. Harryhausen says there's a complete record, although it hasn't shown us the whole thing."

Katie snorted. "Typical. Alien secrecy to protect other aliens."

Jackson shook his head. "It doesn't appear that way, though. Harryhausen says it's not to protect the ones who did it, but to protect G. There's a chance he could recover even more, and he might need those records untouched when he does."

"So why the humming, singing, or whatever he's doing?"

Jackson laughed. "Apparently it's how he survived. The interrogation triggered a memory, and G just fixated on that song. Harryhausen says there's evidence that the song *infected* the torture instruments. They were all flashing and blinking in rhythm. G went to his Happy Place and it saved him. The fucking bastards drove him insane with whatever they did, and we still don't know why."

The dropship pilot looked over at Ginzberg, polishing glassware. He didn't appear to be looking at anything in particular, just hummed and wiped the glassware. "He seems sane enough, after all, he's working here."

"Nope, the dude's broken. He's gone through insane to the other side and now he's...extremely rigid. Harryhausen said to call it 'enasni.' Damned Wrogul humor."

"He's functional..."

"...and he may yet recover even more, but he can't be a merc anymore."

They sat in silence for a long time, when suddenly Katie laughed out loud. "Oh, oh. Oh! *The song*. Small World! He infected the instruments with an *earworm* and it broke the interrogation!"

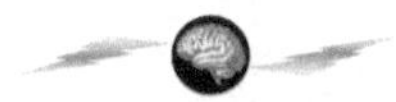

UNTO THE LAST, STAND FAST

Authors note: Chronologically, this is the first of my 4HU stories, and it doesn't involve Wrogul at all. On the other hand, the Custode Sviss will be very important to later events in the Wrogul's Oath. Here, then, is a very different story. If you listen closely, you may recognize a piece of history as well as a Sabaton song.

"Father Salvatore. You have a message?"

"Yes, Your Excellency. My contact says they can get me into the Arritim city. They don't guarantee that I will get out."

"Indeed. The Zuul. They have besieged the city."

"My contact says that the Zuul are not much of a threat. Their lines have too many holes and only one hundred mercenario to fill them. They are unable to use the heavy equipment that was liberated from Zaragossa. They are little better than bounty hunters...eager but not very competent."

"Then we still have a chance to get the Holy One out?"

"Not likely. The Arezzo General Pompe'oCo has brought his own troops, but they are restless. They threaten to sack the city, but for now, Pompe'oCo holds them in check with the Zuul. My contact is not sure how that will last, the mercenario are outnumbered ten-to-one."

"Dire circumstances, then. We are not a rich colony, and Nuova Roma can only authorize a small amount. We have found an agency from Schweiz that specialize in 'Executive Protection.' We cannot afford them, although we have someone who may assist. Even one company is beyond us, for they are Terran and use 'CASPers,' as I think they are called."

"If we cannot afford them, then it matters not if they are even Zaragossan discards, which the Zuul possess, but cannot use. My fear is that the Arezzo might."

"We have a chance at the Schweiz Company, Salvatore. I will send a gentleman with you to Commu'neDi. Mr. Jefferson has been helpful in negotiations with the mercenario. You should have two weeks. The mercenario cannot be here before then."

"Wait, you said we could not afford them!"

"There is more than money of interest to warriors. We have arranged a 'deal' if you will."

"A deal? No, I will not inquire further, you would only dissemble. Yet may I ask how many? I will have the Arritim prepare a passage for them."

"Ah, you wound me, Salvatore!"

"Merely the truth, your Excellency. No more than is right for the Church."

"It is good that you understand, Salvatore. More mercenario than the one hundred Zuul, but not by much. Around two hundred."

"One-hundred eighty-nine, perhaps? Of the Mercenario Sviss? I have heard of this legend. Perhaps the Heavenly Father makes a joke at our expense."

Frank Jefferson turned so that he did not have to see his wife's face as he packed. It was only a small bag; where he was going, he would need only lightweight clothing. If the plan worked, the rest of his gear would meet him on-site. If the plan didn't work, it wouldn't matter, so either way, there was no point in taking too much.

Betsy was crying now, silently, except for the occasional sob. As he sealed the final pouch and applied the device to the valve which would suck all of the excess air out of the package, he turned and took her face in his hands.

"I have to do this, my love."

"No, you don't. Franklin Washington Adams Jefferson, you told me you gave up that. You gave it up for me and to 'buy the farm' you said."

"Betsy Jefferson, I am doing this for you. If this goes badly, there will be no farm, and you will be in danger."

"But it's not your job to defend the Stars or their church!"

"I swore an oath, Betsy."

"Not to them! It's not even your Church!"

"No, my love, I swore it to you. Love, honor, cherish, defend and protect, 'til death do us part."

"If you love me, you'll say no!"

"Ah, but love is only one of the terms, my heart, I promised to cherish, defend and protect. I would not be protecting you if the War comes to San Pietro."

"What can one man do?"

"Not one alone, but my Company will be there."

"And you? Why do they need you if they have the Company? You promised me that you left that behind."

"It is duty, Betsy, duty and love. 'Greater love hath no man than this that a man lay down his life...' for his friends, for his love, for his God, for his home."

"Promise me you'll come back."

"I can only promise to Stand Fast, my love. Unto the Last."

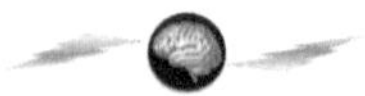

"You know, Padre, I for damn sure wouldn't mind heading to the damned 'Star' city if it wasn't so damned wet!"

"Patience Mr. Jefferson, patience....and please temper your tongue."

Frank just gave a snort of disgust and sat down on the edge of the PlasForm dock attached to the last solid ground for miles. He took off his shoes and hung his feet down into the warm water. He didn't see any crocagators floating in the still water, and this close to the Stars' waterlogged city, there would be few aquatic predators with a taste for human.

Aside from the long peninsula they'd walked in on, they were surrounded by wetlands—bogs, marshes, swamps, trees and open water. On Earth this might be called 'bayou' or 'canali.' On San Pietro it was simply called 'The Wet.' Any human traveling to The Wet knew to dress for heat, humidity and frequent rain. Thus, Frank wore short pants, a loose sleeveless shirt and a hat with a floppy brim to keep the sweat and water out of his eyes. Despite his complaining and the heavy pack on his back, Frank was perfectly comfortable in the light rain, sitting with his feet in water almost to his knees.

Father Salvatore, on the other hand, just *had* to be uncomfortable in his vestments, light weight as they were. He was a big man, and the cassock covered him from head to toe. It didn't look like it was waterproof, either, which meant it had to weigh a ton with absorbed water. However, the only sign that he even noticed the humidity and rain was occasionally removing his glasses to wipe away the water droplets. His face was calm, and he continued to stand at the edge of the dock, looking out along the narrow canal leading to the Arritim city.

Frank noticed a faint ripple, about a quarter klick down the waterway. As it approached, he could see the characteristic 'V' shape of a boat wake. As it approached the dock, the vessel raised slightly out of the water. It was open at the top and filled with water inside. The Arritim communities were largely aquatic, thus their conveyances remained open to the water except for the minimum streamlining required to reduce resistance. The boat—if it could be called that and not a submarine—rose up to the level of the dock and approached to within a few decimeters. There was a driver and one passenger. Much the same as Frank's own party, but while the passenger and Father Salvatore could converse; Frank had little in common with the boat driver, and nothing to say in this meeting. His role would come later.

The passenger rose and stepped out of the water-filled interior onto the dock. He bowed and offered a 'hand' to the Padre. Salvatore, on the other hand, dropped to one knee and kissed the large ornate jewel affixed to one digit of the alien appendage.

"Your Eminence."

There was clearly some form of starfish in the aliens' developmental past, hence the nickname 'Stars' for individual Arritim. The three upper appendages—two 'arms' and a 'head'—were conical projections from a circular central body. Each ended in small boneless digits—and yes, there were ten per limb. Frank knew from the colonist database that the digits on the 'head' were specialized sensory organs, while the ones of the arms served the same function as fingers. The lower limbs were hidden within a garment that looked remarkably like water-filled coveralls, reminding the human colonists of pictures of Old-Earth farmers. Most of the central body, containing the mouth, brain and respiratory organs, was concealed beneath the fluid, but a pair of eye stalks poked out above the surface and continuously scanned the area. The digits of one limb held a small plas-and-metal object, and from this issued a synthesized voice.

"Rise, Father Salvatore, and be at peace. Tell me, what do you hear from Nuova Roma?"

"Thank you, Your Eminence. The news is mixed. The Terran Holy See remains adamant that the Soglio di Pietro remain on Earth and threatens excommunication of Nuova Roma. Even though His Holiness emigrated to Nuova Roma, the Terrans have declared the Stellar Catholic Church heretical. They have their own troubles, and can do little to assist us. We have arranged for a single company of mercenario, and must find a way to get them into Commu'neDi when they arrive."

"That is unfortunate, Teofilo. My source tells me that the Arezzo General Pompe'oCo brought a thousand souls to discipline us, but cannot control them. It would be most regretful if Rome chose to do the same."

"These are turbulent times. The Terran Church senses that it is losing influence. There are those who protest that the races of the stars—even humans—cannot be of true faith for they have never trod the same ground as the

Savior. The Holy See has many cardinals who are ready to agree and declare us *all* heretics."

"It is much the same with us. The General has been calling for the return of the Epichysis and the Telum for several years now. He has been telling the Commons that Arrita'yTer has 'stolen the history' of the Arezzo homeland.

"Dark days, then. He has over a thousand in his force. How can we resist?"

"'At least a thousand souls' according to the reports. Of course, I fear for their souls if they are following Pompe'oCo. I have dealt with him before, and he owes his allegiance to the highest bidder, and not any Divine Direction, no matter what his propaganda says. There are rumors that he has not paid his mercenaries, either. If he does that to his followers, they will revolt."

"In that case there is no more time to waste. I must get into the city, see the Holy One, and then we must prepare accommodations for our own mercenario." Salvatore turned to Frank. "Bless you for indulging an old priest Mr. Jefferson. If you are ready?"

"Oh, not so fast, Father, I have to go, you do not." Frank stood and reached into the heavy bag he'd carried down from the human settlement. He pulled an underwater breathing system that he would need for the trip in the Arritim 'boat.' I promised Bishop Crunelli that I would send you back. He'd never forgive me if I lost you."

"Ah, the impetuosity of youth. You may have me in years, but I know my duty, as well as you know yours, my son." The priest set his legs, and stared at Frank.

"Yes, of course." He reached into his pack and pulled out a second rebreather. "I promised I would send you. I never promised you would go." With that, he handed over the mask and offered the priest a hand to help him into the watercraft."

Father Salvatore's lined face crinkled into a grin. "Ah. Shall we go then?"

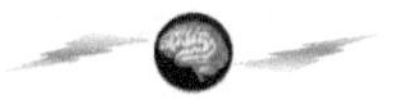

Frank tried to hide his unease as he waded down the 'street.' He and Father Salvatore had been in the city for over a week, and he'd long gotten over both amazement and feeling conspicuous, but tonight would be a bit different, and Frank's mission was critical to their own safety, let alone success. Father Salvatore was conspicuous in his cassock and vestments, yet human seafarmers were common enough that Frank was able to pass relatively unnoticed through the shallow canals that formed the thoroughfares of the alien city. The Stars averaged a few inches shorter than most humans, and preferred water to what would be waist level if they were human. Thus, the pedestrian walkways were about hip deep to a human, and easily accessible to the San Pietro colonist.

He was dressed in typical clothing for those who worked the sea platforms—a tight fitting singlet from mid-thigh to shoulders that kept the water out and his unexposed skin dry, topped by a mesh 'shirt' and head scarf to filter the sun. His feet were clad in lightweight neoprene moccasins that provided traction without adding weight or getting waterlogged. Unlike the humans, nearly all of the Arritim lived in Commu'neDi. Humans on the other hand lived in many places, the cool dry uplands, the hot, humid coast, the deep-sea platforms, and now the archipelago and shallow seas near the Arritim city. They were adaptable, and Frank's clothing reflected that adaptability to the point that he was actually pretty comfortable despite the heat and humidity.

Frank was still a bit bemused at the human and aliens sloshing through the water around him. Even though it happened decades before he married Betsy, 'bought the farm' and settled on San Pietro, it still hadn't been that long since the human colony and the Arritim had been at war over perceived 'invasion' of their colony worlds. The truth was that both colonies were planted at the same time, and the two races would not even have known the other was present except for a chance encounter. The archipelago and shallow seas around Commu'neDi were far enough from the settlement of San Pietro that it would have been decades before the humans ventured that far. To make matters worse, the two colonies were meant to be religious sequesters, and finding *aliens* in their respective hermitage had led to the short Heretic Wars. Only when an Arritim Prisoner of War discovered common ground with a San Pietrese priest, was a settlement reached. The peace turned into alliance and even friendship on common religious grounds—an issue which irritated the respective home churches on both Terra and Arezzo, the Arritim home world, leading to the current unpleasantness.

He reached his destination and entered the building through the water-level doorway. Like most Commu buildings, it was low, but wide, with three levels: one completely under water, the entry level half-filled with water to the same depth as the canals, and an upper level that could be kept dry for storage or human use. The Arritim used all levels, although humans preferred to get out of the water. A few buildings even had additional or enlarged upper floors to accommodate the humans with business in the city. This particular building filled a city block and had a roof access. Frank quickly moved to the uppermost level and looked out over the city. He could see the evidence of the siege off on the horizon—dark shapes and ripples from the submerged platforms. Occasionally there was a wisp of smoke, but that was probably from the Zuul, neither the Arritim nor their Arezzo cousins had much use for fire. There was also no need for Frank to hide from their own view of him; the Arezzo barely acknowledged that the uplanders existed, except to condemn their corrupting influence on the Arrita'yTer religion. Their biggest blind spot was anything more than a few meters above water—a fact that Frank and the Father had counted on for getting their own mercenary reinforcements into the city. He'd wait until dusk, then light the infrared marker for the stealth shuttle delivering the first of the Mercenario Svizz, as Father Salvatore called them.

As darkness fell, Frank could see the green beams and white tracers as the surrounding Zuul and Arezzo fired off their weapons. The last week had been filled with rumors—mostly that Pompe'oCo was losing control. The weapons fire seemed to be increasing, and suggested that there was some truth to the rumor. It was fully dark when he heard three clicks through the waterproof radio he was wearing under his head scarf. Even though he was toward the edge of the roof, he moved even further out such that the roof access was between him and the designated landing zone. A brief rush of wind and a shimmer in the air heralded the arrival of the stealth shuttle. After some muffled sounds and indistinct movement on the rooftop, one shadow separated itself from the others and came up in front of Frank.

"For the Grace, for the might of Our Lord" spoke Frank.

"For the Faith, for the Way of the Sword" replied a voice with the countersign. "I'm Captain Riedel. You are?"

"Frank Jefferson. I've been sent to meet you." Frank peered out at the still indistinct shadows moving on the rooftop. The Captain had night vision optics pushed up on his head, so the others probably had the same. "I see a maybe a platoon. Where are the others?

"Oh, hell no, this isn't even a platoon. The shuttles aren't big enough."

"A Mark Nine can handle two platoons and gear."

"We're not using Mark Nine's anymore, 'Prez.'"

Frank whirled to face the person behind him. He was about to lay into the newcomer for using that handle until he recognized the face behind the voice. His face lit in a smile. "Steel? How'd they drag your sorry ass down here? And why aren't you using Mark Nine's?"

Nicholas "Steel" Stihl laughed. "Same as you, I guess. I hadn't expected to see you here, either, Prez."

"Actually, I live here now. I 'bought the farm.'" He paused a moment, then clarified. "Colonization credits. Betsy wanted forty acres and a mule. They haven't decanted all the mules yet, but we've got a spread up in the mountains where it's cooler and drier."

"Betsy, huh. So, she waited for you. Lucky dog. Oh, and a farm sounds nice right about now."

"Yes, but you haven't answered my question. Why aren't you using Mark Nine shuttles? I cleared a landing zone expecting at least a Mark Eight or even O-I-V's!"

"We don't have them. The Company's not in great shape. We were on the wrong side in Zaragossa, lost half of our men, most of our CASPers. Your 'forty acres and a mule' are why most of us are here. One last job to earn colonization credit and then get the hell out of this life."

"Umm, okay. I didn't realize that was the Company at Zaragossa. On the other hand, I might know how you can get some of that equipment back..."

"Gentlemen. Focus," the Captain interrupted. "We need to secure a perimeter, secure the Principal, clear the area inside the perimeter, and then determine exfil. Once we get the Headquarters platoon down the Major can fill you in." He paused, as if listening to something. "Oh. That's f—-ed up. The Zuul have filed protest and Breach of Contract. The General has lost control of his mob."

Raising his voice slightly, he spoke to the troops on the rooftop: "Mission change. We need to get the rest of Second platoon down *now,* with First and Third down by daybreak. Clear the shuttle and send it back up. McCarthy! Alpha Squad arm up and on me." Turning back to Frank he explained. "The Major has been monitoring the Guild channels. He was expecting something like this. It just means we accelerate the schedule and we *are* bringing everyone down tonight. I think we'd better go see your Holy One right away."

Steel grinned. "So, does this mean you're back in the game, Colonel?"

The captain's head whipped around at the mention of the rank. "Colonel? What? Who?"

Steel pointed to Frank. "Lieutenant Colonel Franklin Washington Adams Jefferson. Call-sign 'Prez' since he was named for presidents of the old US of A."

"Full Colonel, Steel; and Benjamin Franklin was never President."

"Sure, but at least he got his face on the hundred-credit chit."

"Your Holiness, please keep your head down" Major Christopher DiNote told the Arritim priest. "We cannot be certain that there are not snipers within the city already."

DiNote, Jefferson, and the human and Arritim priests were on the top floor of one of the few three-story buildings in the city. The balcony was designed to not only provide a commanding view of the city, but also to provide the city with a view of the occupants of the balcony. It was this latter that concerned the mercenary commander.

For a race that has little use for fire, they are certainly embracing it now, Frank thought. Columns of smoke rose from several points around the perimeter of the city. In a purely human city, there would be shouting and crowds in the streets. The Stars had a high ululation instead of shouting, but it was largely inaudible to the humans. The depth of water in the streets had deepened as levees at the edge of town were damaged by the besieging army, making passage more difficult, but keeping the crowds down. Still, the locals were resisting to the best of their ability— the Arritim had changed more than their racial name when they left their homeland on Arezzo—they had no desire to submit once again to their distant cousins. In all, though, it was a remarkably quiet siege, save for the sound of distant weapons fire, and the occasional ricochet or stray projectile shot.

The priests had wanted to come up to the balcony to assess the conditions in the city themselves. As was fairly typical for both holy "men" they disregarded the risk to themselves, leaving that worry to Frank and the Major. A slight "tink" sound caught the Franks attention, and he looked down to see a deformed fragment of metal. He picked it up and held it out in his palm for the priests to see.

"Father Salvatore, Patriarch Clement, you really need to take cover. This is a railgun projectile. It's spent, which means the range was too far, but that won't be the case for much longer. We need to get you to cover before the skirmish lines ...sooner rather than later.

Frank awoke in the dark. He blinked twice, and the chrono display in his contacts showed the time: 0423. *Oh-Dark-Thirty.* So, he'd been asleep for two hours. Mediating the argument between the two priests and the mercenary commander had taken them well past midnight. Two hours' sleep was enough to take the edge off of fatigue, but it wasn't *real* sleep...that or he'd gotten soft in his years as a farmer.

Something had awoken him, though, and as he searched his memory, he realized that he'd heard a squishing sound, similar to that made by water-filled boots. *Arritim? Or Arezzo?* He blinked, and then squinted, activating the night-vision mode of his contacts. *Strange, he hadn't worn a chrono in years, let alone a tactical vision system. He'd* liked *being out of the game, but apparently; the game wasn't out of him.*

Without moving, he scanned the room. *There!* It was one of the Stars alright, but not armed. The threat-detection readout in the corner of his visual field was yellow-green, no threats other than the strange presence.

"Colonel Jefferson?" The synthesized voice gave little clue as to the identity of the speaker, but the use of his old rank did. So far, only a few of the Company, Father Salvatore, and the Star's High Priest knew that detail.

"Patriarch." Frank gave the minimum response, waiting for the Holy One to reveal his purpose for disturbing Frank's sleep. "

"Colonel. I do not know these Men of Fire and Flame." The Patriarch continued. I do not know you, but Father Salvatore says you are a good man. I fear for my people. I fear for the Faithful, and am not comfortable with this plan. I should reveal myself to Pompe'oCo and let him take me and spare the city."

Frank sat silent. This was precisely what they had argued so late last night. DiNote favored booby-trapping the main avenues of advance, then setting up a hard line of defense around Patriarch. This would slow down the Arezzo, funnel them into zones where snipers could attrit the forces and smash them against reinforced defenses at the basilica. The priests had argued that the plan was too dangerous to the city's inhabitants. Personally, Frank thought that the Major's plan was ignoring the fundamental axiom of never assuming you had an unassailable position. On the other hand...

"Your Holiness..." Frank began, but was interrupted by a static sound from the Star's translator.

"That title is somewhat doubtful at the moment. Please, just call me Father Clement."

"Very well, Father, but I am not a Colonel at present. Just Mister Jefferson...or Frank." Frank paused a moment, then continued his original thought: "Father, you have no guarantee that surrender will save your people. The Arezzo forces out there are behaving in every manner consistent with fanatics. The General has stirred them up, and they will settle for nothing less than destroying you and your church. You may think you'll save lives by not resisting, but it is my professional opinion that the only guarantee of saving lives is to stop the enemy cold."

The electronic box produced a pretty good emulation of a sigh. Interesting that someone had programmed the translators in such a manner. "You may be right, Mister Jefferson, but I fear for my people. Mine and yours, for Pompe'oCo may not stop with just Commu'neDi."

"His troops won't be venturing up into the high plains, Father. Not easily."

"Not by themselves, but they've demonstrated a willingness to use orbital weapons."

That was true. It was why the full Company was not on the ground, including the CASPers. The shuttle carrying Headquarters Platoon had been shot down. It was next to last, with the CASPers scheduled to come down in the final pass. If Major DiNote hadn't come down as soon as he heard of the Zuul withdrawal; Frank might very well have found himself in command. He had mixed feelings over that possibility. He wasn't sure the Major was taking into account the fanaticism of the enemy, nor the obstinacy of the defenders.

"We need something different, Father. Something no one is expecting..." Frank trailed off. An idea occurred to him. It was something that had been nagging at him since he first heard that the Arezzo were bringing Zuul mercenaries to the planet. It had more to do with where he'd last heard of the Zuul...Zaragossa.

He stood, donned his boots and reached into the small locker at the foot of his cot. He'd brought it. Despite Betsy's protests and his own misgivings, he'd brought his uniform tunic, with the three stars and braid of a full Colonel's rank insignia. "Father, I think perhaps we should wake up the Major. I have an idea, and I suspect I'm going to have to pull rank to get him to go for it!"

"I still say we fort up and make them come to us." The Major was insistent. "We can hold a fixed position against a thousand irregulars, no problem...and it won't even *be* a thousand because we're grinding them down as they work their way to us."

"At the cost of half the city. These people have to *live* here, Major. *I* have to live here when this is done," Frank clarified. "We need to draw them off. Make them think they've won, or at least are winning, and that their main target is not here. It's the only way to get them to leave the city alone."

"How? You just argued the priest out of surrendering himself on the basis that Pompe'oCo will kill everyone even once he has the Patriarch!"

"Misdirection, Sir." That was Steel. Frank had had to give him a brief outline of the plan, since everything would hinge on Steel's platoon. "If the Father is in Pompe'oCo's hands, he has no reason not to sack the city. On the other hand, if he has confirmed intelligence that the Patriarch is somewhere else, he'll pivot his forces to follow, leaving only a token force which we can easily clean up."

That gave the Major pause. He stroked his chin. "...and just how do you intend to get the priests—I assume you mean to everyone out, and not just the Patriarch—out of the city? If you hadn't noticed, we're somewhat surrounded. The Arezzo are aquatic, so underwater is out. Pompe'oCo is no idiot, so he knows that humans would take to the air. We've certainly seen that he has anti-air assets. How are you planning on getting them out?"

"For that, we need the CASPers," Frank said quietly.

"What the Hell?" Major DiNote exploded. "Our CASPers are in orbit! They're Mark 6's, we can't just drop them from orbit!"

"But what if you had Mark 7's?" Frank continued in that quiet voice.

"We lost our Mark 7's at Zaragossa. I thought you were better informed than that, *Colonel*!" The Major spat the rank title in disgust.

"...and who did you lose them to?" Frank was being extraordinarily patient. His face showed neither anger nor apathy, but his quiet demeanor was somewhat unnerving to onlookers.

"We lost them to the damn Zuul when we had to pull out of Zaragossa!" The Major was cooling down at bit, but it was more out of regret at the loss than disgust at the situation. "Damned incompetent Eatees, but we were hired by the wrong side."

Frank waited just a moment before dropping his final point. He wanted to see if the Major would fill in the gaps himself. "Remember the day you landed? The notice of Breach of Contract? "

Light was beginning to dawn in the Major's eyes. "The Zuul..." He swallowed, and turned toward Frank, for the first time with a look of appraisal and respect. "Do you think they still have them?"

"The letter of protest cited lack of payment, divided command, and the fact that the Stars had confiscated the six CASPers that the Zuul had brought with them intending to use as siege engines. They can't operate them, but they can slave them to a common command link." It was Steel's time to fill in the details, even though it was pretty clear that the implications were dawning on his commander.

"What about ammunition, then?" It was an honest question, not a challenge like the Major's former comments. "Surely the Zuul wouldn't have done much to rearm the CASPers. Not that I would trust anything the Zuul would use."

"All we need are small munitions. Grenades, Penetrators, just about anything explosive; HEAT would be nice, but not really necessary, and no long-range or orbital." Frank pulled out a slate with a list of armaments he needed, and handed it to the Major. "Call for a ballistic drop pod, have them place it in the Wet for recovery."

"The 'Wet?'"

"Bayou. Swamps. To the west back where this archipelago starts. We'll need to work from there, anyway."

"Very well, Colonel Jefferson. I expect I shall be relinquishing command to you, then." The Major had removed a small white baton from his belt, and was holding it out to Frank. "I'll have the adjutant draw up the Transfer of Command. Have you considered who is going to operate those CASPers, since my Squad is still in orbit?"

Steel laughed, turned his head and pointed to the control implant jack behind his ear. "That's where my heavy weapons platoon comes in." He turned back to Frank. "Welcome back, Prez. This should be fun!"

The major snorted and Frank rolled his eyes, but he accepted the baton and clipped it onto his belt.

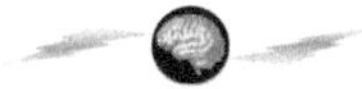

"You want me to *WHAT?*" The disbelief was quite evident in Sergeant 'Bugs' Schmidt's tone, even though no-one could see his face from inside the CASPer.

"It's called the Buckley Maneuver. You launch a penetrator at the rock. You make a hole. You insert a grenade into the hole, back up, and blow the grenade. You drag the rubble out of the way, then rinse, lather and repeat." Steel's voice came from the second CASPer. "I'll be right behind you, breaking up anything too big to remove. If you get a particularly stubborn piece, we'll take it on together. You get a big rock, but you can get past it, do so. I'll take care of it."

"You're crazy, and so is the Colonel! We're below water level, the tunnel will flood!" That was Roeder—aka 'Roadblock'—in the third CASPer, the one tasked with covering their rear, at least until it was his turn to rotate up front.

"Exactly. That's the beauty of it. It carries the heat away when I fuse the walls; it washes out small debris and muffles the sound. We've got pumps for when we're done." Steel's CASPer turned and surveyed the area. A slight pop accompanied the *ping* of a projectile aimed at a crocagator that was getting a bit too nosy. "Now, get digging, Sergeant!"

'Liberating' the CASPers had been easier than they'd predicted thought. It mostly involved getting a squad close enough to enter the Command Override and erase any commands that the Zuul or Arezzo had entered in their attempts to utilize the human equipment. The Zuul had stationed the units in the shallows off-shore from Commu'neDi as part of their original siege line. Most of the Arezzo had long since moved into the outskirts of the city, save for a few technicians who still hoped that they could operate the CASPers. Evolution and intelligence had turned the radially symmetric starfish into a reasonable facsimile of bipedal, bilaterally symmetric humanoid. The main obstacle had been the human counter-intrusion software and compatibility with strictly human brain implants—an obstacle the mercenaries were happy to exploit.

The real problem had not been accessing the CASPers, but rather moving the Combat Assault System, Personal. They didn't dare use the jumpjets, and it wouldn't matter if they had. Zuul mercenaries were not known for meticulous maintenance and upkeep on their *own* technology, let alone something they could barely use. Only one armored combat suit had functioning jets, and three of the six had drained capacitors, one was even missing its cockpit cover and showed evidence of a catastrophic blowout of the ammo magazines. It was obvious why the Zuul had only used them as fixed position cannon—they weren't good for much more than that.

In the end, they'd scavenged canopy, spare parts and ammo, then sunk the three castoffs with thermite grenades on a delayed fuse. The working suits were removed by raft—the same way Steel and his platoon had arrived—to take advantage of the Arezzo's cultural nearsightedness regarding events above water. They'd returned to The Wet and waited for the drop pod carrying ammo, fuel cells, and pumps. Fully armed, and fueled, it was now time to dig.

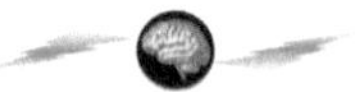

Frank found the priest in the Basilica. It was hard to think of it as a church; it seemed more like an indoor swimming pool with an altar. Most of the humans had left the city, but a few had stayed to join the fight, so Father Salvatore had been hearing confessions from both humans and Arritim. The Arezzo mob had pushed back the Arritim into an area barely three blocks on a side. The Basilica sat on the highest ground of the island which formed the anchor for the mostly-floating city. At that, it was only about 10 meters above water level, but at three stories tall, it had a commanding view of the city...and the fighting. The same height made it a commanding target. Frank and Major DiNote had argued for a more peripheral, less conspicuous hold-out, but the priests had insisted.

"Father Salvatore. Please, it is time to go. Please tell the Patrician that we must ensure his safety."

"Your friends, they are here?" The priest had been showing his age, not to mention the wear of living inside a siege. He'd finally shed the cassock, wearing only the minimal vestments over a light seafarmer's garment. Even the stole and pectoral cross would have to be left behind when they evacuated.

"Not yet, but we must be prepared to move. The mob is getting close. The citizens cannot hold them. They've done enough and we've told them to hide and stay out of sight and be safe. It's up to the Company, now." Frank looked around for the Patrician. "Where is Father Clement?"

"He has gone to retrieve the Holy Relicts. If the Arezzo are indeed a mob, they will likely not recognize the Epichysis and Telum as valuable and destroy them."

"The Epi-whatsit and Telum? A telum is a sort of spear, right?"

"That is correct, Franklin. In this case, a spearhead; it is a true relict—a leftover from another time as well as a crystal formed inside of rock. The Epichysis is a vessel for holding oil, wine or some other liquid. A pitcher. On Earth, some might call it the Sangreal."

"The Holy G—? Um. Yeah. Okay, so that's what this is all about? Mystical artifacts with magical effects?"

"No, only mystery in the ecclesiastical sense. Unlike humans, the Arritim have a complete authenticated history of their church. The Epichysis was used to hold oils for interment rites, and the Telum was used to confirm the death of martyrs. No magic, just a powerful reminder that the Arritim believe in the same Divine Grace as we do."

"If it's so holy, yet so well documented, what's the fuss? Shouldn't they be in the hands of Father Clement's church anyway?" A faint rumbling shook the floor and Frank began to look around as ripples appeared in the water.

"The Arezzo do not think so. While most have rejected the Patriarch, some still feel that the Epichysis and Telum are their own historical artifacts. The rest feel that they symbolize a primitive superstition and should be destroyed and kept out of the hands of 'alien-loving heretics.'"

"O-kay. Now that sounds like what you said Rome was saying about *you*." The rumbling increased; it was now evident as a serious of thumps. Frank took the priest's arm and guided him to the edge of the room. "So, which side does the General fall on?"

"According to Father Clement, he wears the veneer of a believer, but his true motivation is to eliminate this colony. After all, the Arritim turned their back on their homeworld, and he thinks *that* is the true heresy. He wishes to destroy us, Arritim *and* human."

"Ah. Just another bully, then. I guess that makes my own motivation that much clearer." The water level began to fall, and Frank could see cracks in the floor of the Basilica. "Yup, right on time. Father, your ride is here. You'd better go get the Patriarch and his Holy Grail and get ready to go down that tunnel!"

Steel, Bugs and Roadblock widened the hole and secured the follower line that they laid in place to guide evacuees through the tunnel. They'd given up on keeping water out of the tunnel—the Arritim would be perfectly comfortable in the water as long as there was light, and the few humans would use breath-packs. The only problem was figuring out who would get the fifty breathing systems they'd managed to collect.

"Bugs! You're going back down the tube; take Bravo Squad of Third Platoon on point. Get to the far end and secure it. I'm pulling Second Platoon off of the defense and sending them to guide and guard Father Clement and Father Salvatore. Frank looked around and counted mentally, Bravo was ten, the platoon another thirty, plus the human priest. "And...we have 8 more civilians; give them breath packs and flashlights. Captain Riedel, get your platoon and the civilians down that line. There's one more breath-pack; Major, I think that needs to be you."

"No, Colonel, as the senior officer, you have to preserve Command."

"Not me, Major. Wrong choice. The men don't know me other than as a plaque on the wall or stories told in a bar. Besides, I'm not active duty. If someone's going to make it through this and collect on behalf of the Company, it needs to be you. No argument. Go!" Frank paused a moment, and looked at the second CASPer. "Roadblock! As soon as the last person goes down the tunnel, block off this end. You're the road-block for real."

As Frank turned toward the exit, he was stopped by the surprisingly gentle touch of the armored limb of the third CASPer. Steel's voice came over the comm implant that Frank still wore despite years away from the Company. "You realize that when Second pulls off of the line, it's going to weaken. We might not be able to hold."

"Then we hold long enough for Roadblock to collapse this end of the tunnel."

"That was pretty novel idea, having us dig a tunnel."

"Not really, I got the idea from some books I read and a song I heard when I was young. Besides, the Stars pretty much *only* think about open water. They know that humans utilize the surface and the air above, so they would've expected us to make an aerial escape. Only a desperate man would tunnel underground, and the Stars could *never* conceive of tunnels inside solid ground. It worked."

"He's got a guard of forty-two..."

"...along a secret avenue. You heard that song, too. How many left outside?" Frank asked.

"One hundred fifty-five, plus you and me," came the reply over the comm.

"Okay, then, history repeats. We're the One Hundred Eighty-Nine, and there's no question but that we're in the Service of Heaven!" In a quieter voice, he added, "and the General is just one more bully that needs to be stopped. For our homes and families."

Frank stepped out the front door of the church, and positioned himself at the top of the stairs leading down to the water. He pitched his voice to activate the Company comm channel.

"Gentlemen. Time to stand fast."

A mixed group of humans and Stars gathered in front of the ruined church, it's far long since extinguished, and the stains of blood and soot long washed away by the frequent rains. Father Salvatore and Father Clement stood directly in front of the obelisk on which were inscribed, starting from the top, one-hundred and fifty-five names, and then further down, another forty-two names were added to the memorial so that all would remember the sacrifice of the Company.

Major DiNote knelt in front of Betsy, presenting her with both the flag of the Schweitz Company, for Frank's service, and the American Flag for his country of birth. "For no greater love...In grateful remembrance." The words had changed, for few nations claimed the obedience of those who fought on their behalf.

Schmidt and Roeder stood at attention in full uniform to either side of the priests. Their uniforms bore two new devices: The Christian Cross symbol bisected by a spear point on a field of red, gold and blue signified that they were now members of the Arrita'yTer Guardians. A smaller version served not only as a campaign ribbon on the uniforms of the surviving members of the Company, but also signified that they were now landowners on San Pietro. Major DiNote had received the necessary release to muster out all survivors and then reconstitute the guard force under the employ of San Pietro in exchange for their land-grants. In a very real way, all one-hundred and eighty-nine had 'bought the farm.'

After the ceremony and brief homilies by both human and Arritim priest, Father Salvatore took DiNote aside. "One thing I never asked, Franklin was neither Deutsch nor Schweitz. How did he come to be part of the Mercenario Sviss? You yourself are...Italiano?"

"Ah, yes. Well, I suppose you'd have no reason to know. We're not all from Schweiz Colony. In fact, most of us enlisted for Colony Credits. Neue Schweitz could take a few, and others could cash out and invest in Terran Outbound—land grants as long as you swear to defend them. That's what

Frank did...how he ended up here...and why he felt obligated to fight." The Major, soon to be Captain General of the 'Custode Sviss' Executive Protection Company, sighed. "As for me, Italian roots, Catholic even, but I'm from New Jersey. Just like Frank was from Texas."

"So, why do you do it? Why did he do it?"

"As I said to Betsy. 'No greater love.' Sometimes it's the only way to stop an enemy force. Not to mention that there's just something in our psychology that can't abide a bully."

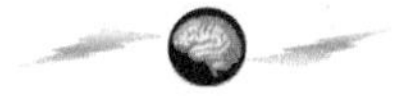

Acknowledgements

I'd like to thank Mark Wandrey and Chris Kennedy for the opportunity to play in the Four Horsemen universe. When I was first invited to contribute to a 4HU anthology, I created a world, alien race and setting of my own. When I was asked for a second time, I asked Mark what to do, and he said "well, you know, there's these octopus-like aliens that implant brain-computer interfaces...sort of like what you do in real life..." With that prompt, I was off and running. Two short stories grew into three, plus three novels and a fourth on the way.

I am greatly indebted to Chris for co-authoring the first novel with me, and helping me flesh out the world of the Wrogul. I want to especially thank Sandra Medlock, for co-creating the world of the Wrogul with me. She's a great co-author and editor. My thanks to William Alan Webb and Jamie Ibson for cover and formatting assistance and advice. To the entire Peacemaker Cantina—I can't think of a better, more supportive, and more educational group of writers. To Chris Kennedy, thanks for bringing us all together and giving me a chance at my first independent publications.

Sandra, Chris, and I created many wonderful Wrogul characters...but Squiddy is all mine!

About the Author

Dr. Robert E. Hampson is a Neuroscientist and author. By day, he is a professor at Wake Forest School of Medicine, studying how our brains encode memory. By night, he writes military, adventure and hard-science Science Fiction as well as nonfiction articles explaining science to the general public.

Robert Hampson's SF writing career began with "They Also Serve," a short story in Riding the Red Horse, published in 2015. That story became the foundation of his first solo novel The Human Side, in 2020. He has three collaborative novels with Sandra Medlock, Chris Kennedy and Casey Moores in the "Wrogul's Oath" arc of the popular Four Horsemen Universe. A final book in this arc is expected in late 2023.

Rob's latest novel is *The Moon and the Desert,* an updated retelling of The Six Million Dollar Man. In addition to novels, he has co-edited two anthologies, and published more than 25 works of short fiction (some written as "Tedd Roberts"). He is also a regular contributor of nonfiction articles for science fiction readers, with more than 15 articles published. One of the articles, "Why Science is Never Settled," was nominated for the Hugo Award in 2015 as Best Related Work. Hampson has sequels in the works to both solo novels, the Wrogul's Oath, and The Founder Effect anthology.

Dr. Hampson's forty-year scientific career has ranged from studying the effects of commonly abused drugs on memory, to the effects of space radiation on the brain. His current work, as lead scientist for Braingrade, Inc., is developing a medical device to restore human memory function damaged by injury or disease. He is also a professor of physiology/pharmacology and neurology at

Wake Forest School of Medicine where he teaches regularly in the neuroscience and biomedical graduate curriculum. He also developed and teaches a course on Communicating Science, in which young scientists practice writing for—and speaking to—the general public. He is a scientific journal editor; a reviewer for dozens of journals and research agencies; has been interviewed on his research by newspapers, radio and TV; a consultant to TV and game producers, defense contractors, and authors. He has published more than 175 peer-reviewed scientific articles.

Hampson graduated in 1988 with a PhD from the Bowman Gray School of Medicine of Wake Forest University in Winston-Salem, NC. He has worked as a newspaper carrier, greeting card merchandizer, computer data entry operator and programmer, and laboratory technician, and lived in Pennsylvania, Texas, and North Carolina. He now lives in the Piedmont of North Carolina with his wife, Ruann.

Robert E. Hampson is available as a consultant through SIGMA — the Science Fiction Think Tank and the Science and Entertainment Exchange (a service of the National Academy of Sciences). His website is .

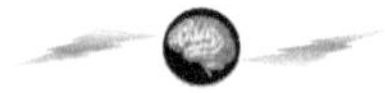

Books by Robert E. Hampson

The Moon and the Desert - Baen Books

ISBN 978-1-982192-49-5

What would it really take to make the Six Million Dollar Man? a medical thriller on earth and in space!

Glenn Armstrong Shepard had his sights set on going to Mars as a flight surgeon, but a training accident on the Moon left him crippled. Now he has a new plan: to be fitted with bionic prosthetics and come back even stronger.

Fate and the Space Force have other plans, and Glenn is grounded. Another doctor—his ex-fiancée—takes his place, and Glenn will have to fight to prove he can be an astronaut once more. . . .

The Human Side - Theogony Books

ISBN 978-1-648550-70-6

Is it an asteroid...or a weapon?

An asteroid headed toward Earth was not unexpected; multiple asteroids were a different story. And, when the "rock-throwing aliens" finally appeared, the people of Earth had to deal with a new type of war, where an enemy with powerful weapons held the high ground of space.

Dr. Tobias Greene felt guilty over patching up soldiers only to have them return to battle—until learning that his work was essential to the survival of the human race.

Master Sergeant Martin was a combat medic, trying to do his job and save as many as he could.

Lab Technician Kat Smith was forced out of her home and away from friends and family by the alien attacks. Her work was important, but would it be enough?

Jan and Li Janacek were trapped in New Mexico with their son, daughter, and eight other teens. They needed to get home...but home was no longer there.

For Arielle French, the aliens' arrival was everything she had predicted, until they attacked. Had she misunderstood their motives, or was it all the fault of the humans who failed to behave the way the aliens expected?

Technical breakthroughs might allow humans to resist the worst the "Rockers" could throw at them. But even if they could level the battlefield, though, would there be enough time left for Earth to show the Rockers what was really on the Human Side?

The Founder Effect - Anthology (edited with Sandra L. Medlock) - Baen Books

ISBN 978-1-982125-09-7

AWARD-WINNING AND BEST-SELLING AUTHORS CON-TRIBUTE NEW STORIES: All-new fiction from Dragon Award winner and New York Times best-selling author David Weber, Dragon Award nominee D .J. Butler, best seller Jody Lynn Nye, indie best sellers Chris Kennedy and Mark Wandrey, and more. Also featuring an introduction by multi-award-winning and New York Times best-selling author Larry Correia.

It is 2185 CE. Humans now live throughout the Solar System, but their most ambitious adventure is about to begin. The starship Victoria will carry over 10,000 colonists to a new world outside the Solar System. The larger-than-life exploits of those colonists will become legendary. The colonists will build a new civilization, and the actions of a few individuals will become famous—and infamous—forever marking their new colony with the Founder Effect.

Contributors: Larry Correia, Mark H. Wandrey, Les Johnson, Christopher L. Smith, David Weber, Daniel M. Hoyt, Brad R. Torgersen, Monalisa Foster, Sarah A. Hoyt, Chris Kennedy, Vivienne Raper, Jody Lynn Nye, Brent M. Roeder, Catherine L. Smith, Philip Wohlrab, D.J. Butler

Stellaris: People of the Stars - Anthology (edited with Les Johnson) - Baen Books

ISBN 978-1-481484-25-1

NEW STORIES AND ESSAYS FROM TOP AUTHORS AND EXPERT SCIENTISTS. Explorations of how interstellar travel may affect humanity by best-selling authors and scientists.

The stars will change us.

STELLARIS: PEOPLE OF THE STARS is a collection of original science fiction stories and nonfiction essays speculating about humanity's far-term expansion into the universe beyond the limits of our solar system—with an emphasis on the changes humans will undergo as a species as we make this happen. Is interstellar travel so far beyond our current imaginings that it will take a fundamental transformation of humanity in order to make it possible? And, if so, will we remain Homo sapiens or become a new and unique species—Homo stellaris (the People of the Stars)?

Herein are original science fiction stories by award-winning authors such as Kevin J. Anderson, William Ledbetter, Todd McCaffrey and Sarah A. Hoyt, supplemented by accessible nonfiction essays describing the science behind the fiction from people who should know—Sir Martin Rees (Astronomer Royal of the United Kingdom), Mark Shelhamer (Chief Scientist for the NASA's Human Research Program), and more.

This collection of original stories and essays was inspired by a gathering of scientists, science fiction authors, and futurists at a series of annual meetings held by the Tennessee Valley Interstellar Workshop. Let their speculations, imaginations and boundless sense of what's possible take your own journey beyond the edge of the solar system in STELLARIS: PEOPLE OF THE STARS!

Stories and Provocative Speculation from:

Sir Martin Rees, Kevin J. Anderson, Sarah A. Hoyt, Mike Massa, William Ledbetter, Todd McCaffrey, Kacey Ezell and Philip Wohlrab, Dan Hoyt, Les Johnson, Robert E. Hampson, Mark Shelhamer, Brent Roeder, Jim Beall, Cathe Smith

The Wrogul's Oath

Do No Harm (Robert E. Hampson and Chris Kennedy with Sandra L. Medlock)

ISBN 978-1-950420-11-7

When Todd's critically damaged ship dropped out of hyperspace near the Human colony world of Azure, he had no memory of his past. He didn't know who he was, or even what he was, and the Humans didn't either. That didn't stop the colonists of Azure—they took him in, anyway...even though they didn't understand how he could do some of the things he could do.

Todd and his descendants consider themselves Human—eight armed and water-breathing—but Human, nonetheless. After seventy years living among Humans, Todd's descendants are going back out into the Union to make their mark—from fifteen-year-old Verne, who's a little short to be a mercenary, to Harryhausen, who wants to be the most famous PI in the galaxy. Eventually they learn that the rest of the Galactic Union knows them as Wrogul, intelligent octopus-like beings known for science and the ability to perform surgery like no other race can.

These Wrogul do more than just practice medicine, but they still intend to do no harm. Unfortunately, the Humans, whether they have two arms or eight, have powerful enemies... and the Wrogul may have no choice.

And Break It Not (Robert E. Hampson and Sandra L. Medlock)

ISBN 978-1-648551-92-5

The planet of Azure is nearly idyllic—there is a high standard of living, industry is booming, and the two races—Human and Wrogul—get along well with each other most days.

But underneath it all, there is tension between the races. Despite having no reason for it, the Humans don't always trust the Wrogul, and there is a faction within the Wrogul community that doesn't want its young growing up "Human."

When a large group of Wrogul move into the ocean and strange things begin happening—weird lights seen in the depths and sabotage at the mariculture stations—the Human's distrust becomes outright suspicion of treachery.

As things spiral out of control, another force enters the system—a group ostensibly sent by the UN on Earth to inspect the crops being grown on Azure—which threatens to destroy everything the Humans and Wrogul have worked for.

While the Wrogul still intend to do no harm, the Humans have powerful enemies in the galaxy, and, this time, the Wrogul may have no choice about whether to join the front lines with their Human friends. Will the threat of a common enemy break the relationship between the Humans and Wrogul...or break it not?

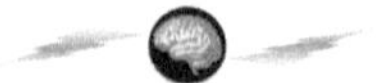

As My Witnesses (Sandra L. Medlock and Casey Moores with Robert E. Hampson)

ISBN 978-1-648554-17-9

Azure Colony avoided the larger conflicts of the Omega War and Guild Wars, only to fall prey to rogue mercenaries. Now they're rebuilding, but strange forces are at work. New friends on the ground and mysterious lights in the sky promise "interesting times" for the Humans and hyper-intelligent Wrogul of Azure.

Meanwhile, mercenary leader Verne and Peacemaker Harryhausen resume their search for the ancestral home of Azure's Wrogul. They encounter distrust, deceit, and misdirection from the all-powerful guilds, but they manage to learn of sightings of Wrogul-like aliens. Their strongest lead takes them to a forgotten system where a lost Human colony coexists with a strange alien race with remarkable similarities to the Wrogul.

But when they find the colony is in the middle of a civil war, they're forced to make a choice—do they choose sides or stand by while the colonists slaughter each other?

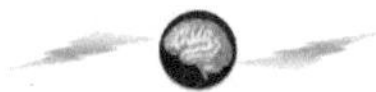

This I Swear (Sandra L. Medlock with Casey Moores and Robert E. Hampson)

Forthcoming in 2023 - the surprising conclusion to Todd's search for his ancestors.

ROBERT E. HAMPSON

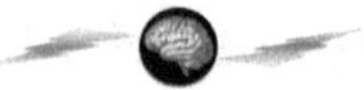